Mystery Among The Trees

Story by Randolph Scott Olson
Written by Dr. Richard A. Olson

LUND FAMILY MYSTERIES

ACTION!
MYSTERY!
ADVENTURE!
FEAR!

The Lund Family Mystery series.

Welcome readers, new, young and not so young.

I, Dr. Richard A. Olson, aka **Dr. Batman**, have the pleasure of introducing you to my Lund family mystery stories. These stories are a spin-off of Scott Lund, the U. S. border patrol agent series. These super adventures focus on Scott's brother Steven, who is tall and powerful. A District Park ranger, and a third-degree black belt in Shotokan. The wife, Scott's sister-in-law is Lorelei, a world class exotic animal veterinarian. She goes by the nickname, Dr. Lori.

One night at the dinner table, The Olson Family had a huddle. Ideas floated around the table and out of thin air, we created the Lund Family characters and what they do and how they act. The trouble they would get into and the mysteries they would solve. It was a blast doing that and made this writer's heart and soul extremely happy for years to come. The making of a legacy.

The Lund children, the actual heroes in these stories are Zac and Zoe. Zac is about 14-15 years old, almost a black belt himself, and a competitive motocross racer. Zoe, the feisty younger sister is a preteen, dances and loves all animals, especially her collie, Rosie.

Both mother Lori and Zoe practice Brazilian Jiu-jitsu.

The first story, **Mystery Among the Trees**, was created by my son Randolph aka Rand; a precocious youth with a can-do attitude. One day Rand came to me and said he wanted to create a story of his own. It was great to collaborate with him and a pleasure to write and put his ideas to paper.

Like father, like son.

We sat down about once every week, he made up the whole thing…the story is funny, outrageous, and dangerous. Whenever I had a question, or wondered which way the story should go, I would ask Rand for advice and direction. The story is his creative thought process, and I respect that fact.

The Second story, Don't Fall In! was created by my daughter Raegan. Her imagination is a treat to behold! Her nickname is Rae. Of course, after big brother Rand created a story, she had to get in on the action. Zoe is in many ways derived from my daughter, Rae with her love and caring, especially with animals. Then add in her energetic personality and look out!

Rae assisted me every step of the way. I would ask her if she knew certain words or not, Sometimes, she would say she knew the word, sometimes she didn't. Or she would say to add the word and thank me for learning it. It seemed that I learned and benefited from writing the story more than she did. During the story we discussed shopping, clothes, meals, movies, and tropical storms. Also, we talked about butterflies, puppies and yes, even snakes. My kind of girl!

Thank God for my wife, Angela, my Angel. The Mother and connective glue of our family and the undercover hero. A woman that works from morning to midnight, doing everything that needs to be done and more! Thanks for putting up with us, our ideas, and supporting your three crazy fun loving writers.

Read, experience, be afraid, and enjoy!

Then let the Olson family know what you think about the Lund family.

Vacation, the stuff dreams are made of or at least the anticipation of the perfect family vacation. Sadly, in today's world most families don't take a vacation. Maybe a staycation at best. But when families do take vacations, they are seldom, if ever, perfect. It would be nice if the family fighting disappeared, the children suddenly were perfectly obedient, no sibling quarrels or fights. The husband and wife would agree in synchrony. No arguments, no disagreements, everybody getting along, the way it should be. But dreams seldom come true. So, let's follow the Lund's on a family vacation and see—just what really happens. A vacation of fun and pleasure or a nightmare of trouble and terror?

You read the story and be the judge. Let's check in on the Lund family.

CHAPTER 1

DAY 1

The ruby red Jeep Grand Cherokee effortlessly climbed up the mountain highway road, due to AWD and the powerful EV engine. The family inside the vehicle looked like an ordinary family, yet much more went on inside than meets the eye.

"Mom, I need more money for Roblox."

The first voice came from a young man, a youth, about 14 or 15 years old, tall, and muscular for his age. Zac's sandy blonde hair that matched Steven's, his father.

A high, almost whiney voice called out, "Mom, can I get money too? It's not fair is Zac gets some and I don't. We're not there yet."

That voice belong to Zoe, and she gets what she wants, or at least keeps trying to. Zoe about twelve, had strawberry blonde hair that had curls on top of the curls. She is average height and had the slender angular body of a dancer, which she was.

"Just give me a minute," said Lori, short for Lorelei. Lori or Mom's fingers were typing on her phone. "I need to finish this text message for work."

Lori worked and owned a veterinarian office based in the U.S and delt with worldwide cases of exotic animals.

A voice loud and shrill sounded from Zoe as most young girls are, "Some Roblox money would be great."

Steven's deep voice sounded out in the confines of the vehicles cabin, "You know how girls are, give Zoe some credits.

Loudly Zoe said, "Thanks Dad, you're the best."

"Dad, tell Zoe to stop yelling." Pleaded Zac, "She always yells."

"I do not yell, I just get excited about things. Are we there yet?" asked Zoe.

Zac wasn't done yet, "You're still too loud."

Looking at the GPS, Steven sighed, "We'll be there in less than an hour."

"See, Mom, some more credits would be great." Sometimes Zac sided with Zoe when it served his needs.

In an exasperated voice Lori said, "Okay, I'm done with my text."

"Lori, make it so." Grunted Steven.

"We are we're on vacation. So okay, have fun."

Both kids chimed in, "Thanks, Mom!"

The hour did go on, and on and on for Steven and Lori...Zac and Zoe quarreled and disagreed most of the way.

Finally, after a long trip, that seemed especially long to the kids, a large wood sign appeared at the side of the road, much to everyone's relief it said, Yosemite National Park. At the top of the sign was a burnt orange arrowhead image, with a green sequoias tree, and white letters saying, National Park Service. A small buffalo and arrowhead were etched at the bottom of the sign.

As the Cherokee turned off the main highway into the park entrance road, Steven announced, "We're here, our vacation has officially started."

Zoe got excited, "When can I see a bear? I mean a bear cub, they are so cute."

"Don't get clawed, sis."

Placing her hands together forming a heart, Zoe said in her high voice, "But they are so cute and furry."

Seeing her heart shape hands, Zac frowned, "Apparently, they don't look like you."

"Mooom! Zac said I'm ugly."

Lori called out, "Zac!"

Without missing a beat, Zac ignored his mother, and asked, "What I want to know is when are we going to see the Grizzly Giant sequoia tree?"

Zoe commented, "Silly brother, bears aren't trees."

An annoyed Zac replied, "It's a nickname for the second tallest tree in the park and the most photographed. It's like over sixty meters tall."

Making a face that wrinkled her nose, Zoe asked, "Are you lying, Zac?"

"He's correct." Stated Steven who is a forest park ranger and oversees conservation duties in the Northwest.

Smiling, Lori's red lips showing off her pearly teeth. She always went to the dentist and has never missed a cleaning. "That will be a great family photo. The Lund's by the Grizzly Giant."

Solemnly, Zac said, "I want a picture of just myself in front of the Grizzly Giant."

"If he gets a solo picture, I want my own too." declared Zoe.

Lori interjected, "We can get as many as pictures we want, but I want a group photo also. Please everybody, just calm down."

Paying more attention to the road, Steven slowed down at the gate, a short line of vehicles were ahead of them. They finally motored to the gate. A kiosk screen displayed, $100.

Steven smiled, "Lori."

Lori opened the center console, took out Steven's wallet and pulled out a green card. Steven inserted the card into the kiosk and took it out. The digital sign changed to green letters that said, *Admit*.

Shifting into gear, Steven drove into the park.

Leaning forward over Steven's shoulder, Zac asked, "How you manage that Dad?"

"Easy, since I'm a Forest Ranger I have an Interagency Pass. One of my many benefits, I can go to any park in the United States free."

With a big smile that showed her dimples, Zoe complemented Dad. "That's so cool of you."

"No, Zoe, it's sick." Zac loved to correct his sister.

"Daaaad!"

Turning around, Lori narrowed her eyes. "Zac your sister can say what she wants."

"Cool, cool, and super cool." Zoe had a smug look on her face.

Zac started to open his mouth, but Dad interrupted him.

"Look at the view gang, isn't it marvelous." Father Steven said trying to keep the peace.

The scenery was indeed spectacular, the giant ancient sequoia trees, the towering waterfalls and the looming granite cliffs of El Capitan and Half Dome. After driving for about an hour they came to Yosemite Village, full of shops, restaurants, lodgings, the Museum and the Ansel Adams Gallery.

Steven looked into the rearview mirror, as Zac started to poke Zoe, he noticed Dad and froze, then gradually moved his hand and pretended to scratch himself. Zac tried to keep a straight face. Dad wanted to laugh, but being a parent, he couldn't.

The Lund's noticed the historic sign which read: "Everybody welcome to Yosemite Park, perhaps the most iconic spot in California. A place too good to miss, I'd go so far to say it's one of the best national parks in North America."

With voice lowered, Steven claimed, "I've been to a lot of parks, too many to count or remember, but this park is worth the visit. Everybody, enjoy our family adventure."

Read more of the story and see what kind of adventure the Lund's will find.

Lori's blonde head turned to the kids, "If your father says the park's the greatest, then it's true."

Sighing, Zac commented, "Maybe Mom, but I'm bored right now."

"Me too." Chimed in Zoe. "boring, boring—bored."

Snapping at his sister to correct her, "Zoe, yours always so bored."

"Stop it! We are here." said Lori in her mom voice. "And--we're going to have FUN!"

They drove around taking in the sights and picking out a place to hike the next day since now too late afternoon to start a hike.

Zac called out, "I need to use the can, like now."

In her high shrill voice, Zoe agreed, "Yeah, Dad I gotta go potty also."

Answering back, Dad said, "Okay, we are close to some Restrooms, Hang on, I'll pull in soon."

They parked and got out to use the facilities, the call of nature would be answered. The family used the facilities for a few moments. After washing up, the Lund's were standing in the parking lot talking about important stuff, like where to go for dinner. Lori and Steven started to get back inside the Jeep. Being hyper, the kids moved about quite in the parking lot.

"Can we get a quick sip of water Dad?" asked Zoe.

Zac added, "It will be okay, I'll go with her."

We're really thirsty." Please Zoe in her cute way.

"Yeah Mom, just a quick drink."

Frowning, Mom thought about it, "Don't take long and come right back. You hear?"
Both kids agreed, and they went to a water fountain by the side of the building. A Border Collie trotted by that must have gotten loose.

Excited by seeing the dog, Zoe chased after it, "It's so cute, It's got a collar, I'll get it."

"Wait sis, stop." Zac called out, "Wait for me."

Waving bye at Zac, Zoe took off.

Of course, she didn't stop and ran after the dog into some bushes.

Calling out again, "Zoe, stop! I am going to get grounded for this. Please come back."

Zac squinted his eyes; it looked like the bushes had gobbled up Zoe.

"Zoe?" Zac called out as he approached the shrubbery. "Zoe! This isn't funny. Get out here now. I mean it!"

Hearing a rustle, Zac saw a dog running out of the bushes ran, its deep brown eyes looked playful, with Zoe following the canine. Since Zoe loved animals she should be along with the dog. Creases appeared across Zac's forehead. "Zoooeee!"

Going to the bushes, Zac pulled back a branch. "Where are you Zoe? You get stuck sis? Get out here--now! I mean it."

Bulling his way into the bushes, like kids do. Zac saw Zoe sitting on her knees. Zac's eyes got so big they were ready to explode. Zoe was kneeling by an object. Not just any object, a human body lay there. The body of a man!

With tear-filled eyes, Zoe looked at Zac pleading for help.

"Zoe, what the…"

Her voice deadly serious, he skin white as a ghost Zoe said, "I, I, didn't kill him. I found him this way. Honest. At first I thought he was asleep, but he wasn't. I don't know what's going on."

Not knowing whether to laugh or not, Zac approached the inert body, his muscles tight and trembling. He bent over the body and placed his hand over the mouth. "He's not breathing."

"I know, I'm afraid Zac. What do we do?"

"Hmmmmm. Let me think about it."

Suddenly in a whirl, Zac hauled off and kicked the man in the thigh, good and hard.

Slam! The sound of hitting flesh could be heard.

With her mouth opened in surprise and shock, Zoe loudly asked, "What…why did you do that Zac? Why would you kick a dead man?"

"I kicked him hard, it can't hurt him if he's dead, and he might have gotten up if he had been sleeping."

"I'm telling Mom you kicked him."

Shaking his head no, "Let's go get Dad."

"Zac, just tell them I didn't do it. I couldn't harm a living creature"

Walking back and still shaking his head Zac was in disbelief as they re-entered the parking lot.

CHAPTER 2

At the sight of their parents by the Jeep, Zoe raced over yelling, "Mom—Dad, we found a dead guy in the bushes."

Correcting his sister, "No, Zoe found a dead man."

Lori said, "What? Are you guys joking? It's time to go, we need to check into our room and get ready for dinner." Then she noticed Zoe's tear-stained cheeks and reddened eyes. "Steven?"

Grabbing Dad's hand, Zoe yanked on it, "C'mon Dad, please, for real there is a dead guy in the bushes."

In a firm voice, Dad said, "Slow down Zoe, tell me what's going on?"
"She's not lying Mom and Dad I saw the body too."

"Zac, you kicked the body."

"No, I didn't."

Zoe yanked harder and harder. She yanked so hard that Dad had to hide a wave of pain. "Yes you did Zac, you kicked him as hard as you could. C'mon Dad—Mom lets go see the body."

Wrinkling her nose, Mom asked, "You kicked a dead body, Zac?"

Raising his right eyebrow, Zac said, "I'm not saying anything, but we should follow Zoe, let's go."

Sternly Steven said, "Okay this is weird, let's go Mom. There must be something to this."

Agreeing Mom gave in, "Okay, we will humor you kids and go look."

So, the Lund's went to the bushes and pushed their way through. What did they find?

Nothing. There was no body ?!?

"It laid here a minute ago." Zoe cried out and pointed to a spot on the ground, "There was a man lying there."

Jumping in, Zac backed up his sister for once, "Yeah, Dad. He didn't seem like an ordinary guy. He was wearing a dark grey suit and white shirt. He looked like some kind of undercover cop."

In a mother like way, Lori placed her hands on her hips, "Are you two telling the truth? Don't lie to us."

"Honest Mom, this is way too big a lie for Zoe and me to tell."

Zoe grabbed Dad for a desperate hug for reassurance, Dad hugged her back, "I'm scared. What if the body came to life and walked off? He could be hiding and run out and eat us."

Dad scolded her, "You've seen too many zombie movies on Netflix, young lady."

"Enough with the zombies." Mom said, "Let's leave and get to our motel room, I want to get cleaned up."

Not wanting to quit, Zac said, "But there was a man lying there is the bushes."

19

"Yeah Mom, I was chasing a lost dog and followed him into the bushes and that's when I found the body."

Upset more than he wanted to admit, Zac said, "That's when I found Zoe in the bush, kneeling by the dead man."

After several minutes of arguing, believe it or not, Steven called the police.

"There are no missing persons or deaths reported for this area." the deputy sheriff stated while scrolling through his tablet. I think your children must have quite an active imagination."

Defensively, Lori responded, "Sometimes the kids lie, but they are not liars. They must have seen something."

Tugging on Mom's arm, Zoe wasn't going to quit, "Mom, I saw a dead body, for real."

"Enough." Mom said "We'll talk about it later.

Agreeing, Zac said, "Mom, we need to find the body, since there was a body there must have been a person who killed him."

Giving a half smile that showed one dimple. It was hard to tell if Zoe was serious or joking. "Yeah mom, there must be a zombie killer."

Correcting his sister, "Zoe, he would be a killer not a zombie killer. The body would become a zombie and walk off."

Putting her finger in front of her mouth, Mom said, "Shush!"

The deputy's ignored the kids' protests, his tone lowered, "Whatever they saw is long gone, I walked the perimeter and came up with nothing. I've had enough of this bull."

Hoping that Steven would say no, the deputy asked, "I don't want to, but I'll file a report if you insist, but only because Mister Lund is a Park Ranger."

Replying in a monotone Steven responded, "I don't want any special favors just because I'm a ranger. I have two good honest kids, there must be a reason for what they are saying. They must have seen something."

"Sir, there is nothing to be found here. Can I be of any further assistance?"

Reluctantly, Steven stuck out his hand, the two men shook; "No, no, you've done your job, but I do want a report filed and any notices of deaths or missing person's to be reported to me."

The deputy slowly shook his head in disbelief as he made his way to the patrol car. "I'll keep my ears open in case a missing person…or zombie is reported and let you know." He mumbled something about kids as he drove away.

"So where does that leave us?" asked Lori.

Zac pleaded, "Dad, can we look some more? We did see a man's body."

Making her patented lower lip pout, Zoe said, "We did Dad, maybe he was a vampire."

"Silly sister, vampires don't walk around in the daylight."

"How do you know? You're not a vampire, are you Zac?"

"No, I not a..."

Mom's voice cut through the air like a whip, "STOP!"

But Zac wouldn't let up, "Dad, can we look around, just a little more? Zoe and I saw a body."

Dad shrugged his shoulders giving in, "Okay, but only for five or ten minutes, Mom's not a happy camper."

"Thanks Dad." Said Zoe.

"Let's go look sis."

Off the two young Lunds went.

Mom said nothing. The Lund's looked and looked and looked.

A high shrill voice yelled. "Over here, over here."

Everybody came over, Zoe stood by a tree stump. Zoe, her green eyes blazed triumphantly, she proudly raised her hand, she was holding a badge, in fact an FBI badge.

Dad smiled at his daughter; after all she had told the truth. "I going to call a Park Ranger buddy and report this.

The Lunds had finished dinner at a restaurant, the kids had fought and argued through most of the meal, making it a miserable time. Even the short trip back to the Hotel had been rough. They did see some deer on the way back, which did get Zoe excited, Zac played on his tablet They parked with dust nearing, the shadows of the trees growing longer and longer. The Lund's got out and returned to their room at the Pine Tree motor lodge.

Once inside the motel room, in a not happy voice, Steven reprimanded them. "Next time we might just eat in the room. I'm not happy with your behavior during dinner—at all."

Shrugging off Dad's comment Zoe said, "So, next time we get pizza in the room."

Chiming in, Zac agreed, "Yeah, pizza party tomorrow night."

Scolding them, Mom said, "That's not the point kids and you know it. Father!?!"

"All right. You kids need to simmer down so we can have some fun. That's what we're here for. Let's salvage rest of the night, have microwave popcorn and stream a movie." Dad went to a travel bag pulled out some popcorn bags and got to work with the microwave.

Zac and Zoe jumped on a bed, Zoe quite eagerly jumped an extra time or two, maybe even three. Mom gave her the look, she stopped. The TV flashed on, and channel surfing started.

23

Shaking her head, gave up and Lori resisted telling Zoe not to jump on the bed. She put her hand on Steven's shoulder and kissed his check as he watched the popcorn bag expand and pop.

In a frustrated voice, Lori said, "What are we going to do with these kids?"

Steven turned and gave her a brief kiss. "Pray positive and plan to get through the teenage years. Then ship them off to college."

Both parents laughed.

On a roll, Steven suggested, "Then we can fly off to Australia and fight kangaroos."

Lori responded, "You can fight them Mister Blackbelt, I'm the veterinarian. I'll fix their wounds, sicknesses…and boo-boo's, and maybe yours too if you lose."

They both chuckled and looked at Zac and Zoe who were contently lying on the motel beds watching TV. The parents had taken away the tablets for the night.

Steven noticed the children. "They look calm now."

Shaking her head, Lori sighed, "I still can't believe that the kids found a dead body."

"I'm actually proud how they handled themselves,"

Lori agreed, "Even as an adult, I'm not totally sure how I would have handled it."

Moving his mouth about, like Steven was trying to digest something, "Its looks like they get all the fun.

24

This sounds like something that would happen to my brother, Scott."

Lori elbowed Steven, "Stop it, your brother Scott's in the U.S. border patrol and he is expected to get into trouble all the time."

"I know, but not everybody gets to rescue the President of the United States, not only once, but Scott rescue's the President life twice. Being a forest ranger is occasionally exciting, but it pales in comparison to Scott's life."

Putting sugar into her voice, "Honey, You-Are-Not a boring husband. You keep me on my toes."

"Thanks babe, you're not so bad yourself…"

A high pitch voice sounded out, "Mom, Dad, come here quick!"

Zac called out urgently, "Before you miss it!"

Dad called out, "Hang on I'll be there in a minute."

"Quick Dad, I don't know how long it will be on the screen." Zoe said quite loudly.

The popcorn was just finishing up, Dad stood still watching the microwave, so the popcorn didn't burn. "Mom."

"On it. What's up?" Mom headed over to the TV.

"Come now and look at the TV." Zac used the remote and turned up the volume.

A TV anchor team was speaking. The announcers were a black man, with a hint of grey in his hair and his partner was a Hispanic woman, about thirty and attractive in a natural way. If she looked any prettier, she would have been the weather person.

"…the missing children's names are Waldo and Alexandra, nicknamed, Lexi. Governor William Meyers had issued a statewide Amber Alert for his two children. Their disappearance was reported yesterday afternoon after hiking in Yosemite Park."

The man spoke loudly and clearly, "The FBI has been called in on the case as well as the local and state authorities. A man hunt has begun combing the area of the park where they were last reported. Now…"

"What did I miss?" Dad was standing by the bed with plastic cups that held fresh smelling popcorn.

The two young Lund's said, "Shuuush!"

Mom added, "Be quiet."

The woman looked at a monitor, her eyes widened. "It has just been reported that an FBI agent named Craig Mulder is missing. His badge number was phoned in to the local Sheriff's department from an anonymous source and turned over to the local authorities. It is feared that FBI agent may be captured or worse yet." Her dark eyes narrowed, "Maybe the agent is deceased? A search for him begins as well."

Zoe looked at her Dad, "That's the badge I found—right?"

Dad simply nodded yes.

A picture of Governor William Meyers and his wife, Carol, flashed on the screen.

The male newscaster paused then went on, "There is a reward for information that would lead to the Meyers's children's whereabouts."

A picture of the two children appeared, a tall slender teenage girl, her blue eyes shined beneath her raven black hair. Next to her stood a younger husky brown haired boy, with freckles decorating the youth's face.

"The children are Alexandra, nicknamed 'Lexi,' her age 15, and Waldo Meyer, age 11."

Camera 2

The female newscaster faked a big smile that seemed out of place. "If you have any information, contact your local authorities about the abductions. We ask for communities to form a network across the state of California to minimize potential delays, avoid confusion and aid all law enforcement agencies in the recovery of the Meyer children. Furthermore…"

Dad turned down the TV volume with the remote control.

Zoe yelled, "What did you do that for?"

For some reason, Zac started laughing.

Dad went over and sat down by Zoe. "It's close to bedtime and I don't want you two all wound up. We can't do anything tonight to help. But I am proud of you with how you handled the deceased body and found the badge."

Falling on his back, Zac kept chuckling and laughing on the bed. Everybody in the room looked at him like he was crazy.

Zoe started laughing along with Zac, but she didn't know why.

Dad glared at Zac, "What's the deal young man, why are you laughing?"

Mom had to get in on it, "This is not funny, a man's possibly dead and two children are missing."

"It's Waldo, Mom, and Dad. The governor's son's name is Waldo. You know, finding Waldo, the game— get it?"

Zoe agreed, it seemed funny, "Yeah, finding Waldo."

Suppressing his chuckle Dad said, "Yes I know the game of finding where Waldo is hiding. But it's getting late, and we had a big day. Listen up Lund family, tomorrow go we find Waldo."

"And don't forget his sister, Alexandra." Zoe said sadly, it seemed she was about to cry.

Mom and Dad sat down by her, and the two parents hugged her. Zac tried to stop his laughing.

It was going to be a long night. Tomorrow the adventure begins for the Lund family, their job is to find Waldo.

CHAPTER 3

DAY 2

Nothing like a family picnic on a sunny day, a few wisps of clouds drifted by overhead. The Lund's packed the picnic table were tons of food, beverages, and of course what young people want--dessert. But at this time the dessert would be the Lund family; gnats, flies, mosquitoes, and bees swarmed about the picnic table.

Swat went Zac's hand. The bug became a squished mesh of goo. The problem being the bug smashed had been swatted on Zoe's left shoulder.

"Zac, you did that on purpose!"

Zac smirked, "No, that mosquito was about to bite you."

Zoe made a face at Zac and swiped at her shoulder, "Mom, Zac hit me."

"I hit a mosquito, not you."

"Mooooom! Zac got goo all over my shirt."

"Somebody had to get the pesky little bug."

"But no on me, you could have let it fly off."

Handing Zoe a wet wipe, Mom simply said, "Stop right now! We came here to picnic and have fun, not fight. Eat your chicken and you two—might get dessert. And—Zac no more swatting bugs when they are on people. Understood?"

"Yes Mom, no bugs on people. Then I'm not responsible if they get bit."

"Mom, I don't want to get bit." Zoe said while swatting at a fly buzzing around her face.

Ignoring all this fuss, Dad pretended to whine, "Can I have dessert, can I? I ate three pieces of chicken. I want apple pie. And..." Giving a broad smile, "I ate all of my veggies, so give me two pieces!"

"Me too." Zac said as he stuffed his mouth with broccoli. Somehow, he kept a straight face. I need two pieces of pie also.

Knowing you two men, I brought along an extra apple pie." Mom went to cooler.

Wanting dessert, Zoe reluctantly ate a bite of chicken.

A group of flies honed in on the food spread out over the picnic blanket. Lori was prepared, she had mesh food covers over most of the items. Nevertheless, the flies snuck in a few morsels. Then a bee decided to attack. Zoe let out a screech as she dived for cover. Dad and Zac picked up linen napkins and started snapping them at the bee, which was joined by another bee. Lori picked up her cup of lemonade and moved under the comfort of a tree, enjoying the two guys ridiculously chasing the bees around. She motioned to Zoe to come over. Zoe did not have to be asked twice. She moved over and stood behind her mother.

"Somehow it seems much safer here Mom."

Napkins snapped and flung about; a bee was down! Zac stomped on it like he was putting out a forest fire. Dad hit another bee, snap! It catapulted down on the blanket, safely landing between the salad bowl and the breadsticks. Steven went to stomp on it.

Watching the men Lori yelled, "No, you don't."

Steven's eyes popped open, his foot froze in midair, the bee flew away. Then Steven spun around and placed his Rocky Mountain hiking boot on the ground. The bee considered itself a victor and flew away to live another day to pester other picknicker's.

Lori marched over to the picnic blanket too reclaim her picnic., "Tell you what gang, let's get dessert down and go for a hike."

Everybody hustled over to eat. They did not have to be told twice.

A few bug swats later, and the dessert, which consisted of fudge brownies and apple pie, was consumed. Afterward, the Lund's policed the camp area and loaded the Jeep leaving virtually no trace behind of them ever being there, except a few fallen insects.

Assembling around Dad for directions, who had out a handheld Garmin GPS Navigator that highlighted a hiking trail. Everyone looked at the course of the trail and nodded in agreement.

Also known as the water cop, Dad said, "Make sure everyone has their water bottles ready and let's get started. About two hours there and two hours back, then we go back to the motel room and get cleaned up for supper. Zoe, do you want to lead, or Zac?"

They both said, "Yes" simultaneously.

And the hike was on. At first Zac and Zoe walked briskly trying to keep ahead of each other. After a kilometer on the trail, Zac was in the lead; his long legs pumping like pistons. Mom called out telling him to slow down. Listening, Zac came to a stop at the top of a ridge and pointed. The family caught up to him and over the ridge down on the hillside were bighorn sheep. About two dozen of them dotted the steep and rough terrain, browsing on grass and clover.

In her high voice, Zoe started to talk loudly about the sheep, "Dad what about…"

Hushing her in a low tone voice, "Zoe let's watch for a moment. We don't want to scare them away."

The bighorns fed, working their way along the ridge. A large ram, with a rack that must have weighed 14 or 15 kilograms led the way. The ewes, and a few lambs tagged along. One ewe kept butting a baby sheep in the behind trying keep up. Trailing a couple of young rams playfully followed suit.

Nodding as the flock moved on, Dad said, "Okay, it's safe to talk."

Zoe commented, "The lambs are cute, can I take one home? Please, Mom and Dad. We could say we are studying them. Mom, you are a veterinarian."

Saying in disgust to his sister, "You would take home a grizzly bear if you could get away with it."

"Well, maybe a small one, then I would train it as it grows up and sick it on you."

Zac gave Zoe a dirty look.

Zoe growled back and raked the air with her fingernails.

Shrugging his broad shoulders, Dad muttered, "I can feel the love."

Mom shook her head at the kids, Mom trained her attention to watching the Bighorns. "You know they were almost extinct a few decades ago, it's great they are flourishing here in the park."

Dad added, "That's right, there might have only been a hundred or so in the late 1990's, today there could be…"

"There are about 2,000 Bighorns now." Zac said, looking at his iPhone screen.

"Could you be more exact brother?" Zoe asked trying to look innocent.

Zac made a sour face.

Mom stated, "While you two were talking they've wandered off." The last sheep's buttock disappeared around the bend.

"Oh well." Zoe shrugged his shoulders and asked, "How about seeing the trees?"

Consulting his Garmen. Dad, the forest ranger said, "We should see some trees soon; we are almost at the Merced groove. There should be a couple of dozen Sequoias there."

"Well let's get it in gear." Mom chimed in.

"Okay, but I'm leading." Declared Zac.

Rather than argue, Zoe took her father's hand and followed.

They climbed another kilometer, reaching the top of the crest, spotted the trees, the Lund's took a water break.

"Wow!" said Zac.

"For once I agree." Releasing Dad's hand Zoe murmured. "It's beautiful."

Moving over to Lori Dad nudge her and Dad pointed at their children. They both smiled at their kids and the beauty of God's nature.

"I guess we should keep them."

Kissing her husband's check Lori said, "Of course dear, they only act up sometimes."

"Can we hike down there a ways? asked Zac.

Adding, Zoe promised, "I'll try not to find any more dead bodies."

"If there is one around we can leave it to you to find it." Zac snorted.

Zoe ignored the comment—this time. "What do you say Mom? Can we take a short hike? We promise not to find any more bodies."

Pretending to frown, Mom said, "Oh, I supposed so, but if you find another dead body you two will be in so much trouble."

Agreeing, Dad slammed his fist into his palm, "There will be tons of trouble for you two."

The whole family laughed and chuckled.

The Lund's are a most interesting family--indeed.

Off went the two intrepid young adventurers.

"There go the kids. Lori, want to make out?"

"Oh, Steven don't you ever stop?" Lori kissed him briefly and Steven tried to kiss her again.

"Eck!" Lori playfully pushed him back, "We better keep an eye on the kids."

"I suppose so, what's the odds of them getting in trouble again?"

"With your family, you never know. Your brother Scott is the world leader for getting into trouble."

"And he gets out of it just as well. You never know when he might save another President or the leader of some third world country."

"You better stay out of trouble yourself there, Steven." Lori laughed, "No rescuing Presidents, do you hear?"

Shuffling his feet and looking down, "You just never know...you just never know."

A high-pitched scream echoed up the ridge. Both parents cried out, "Zoe!" As they raced down the hill.

Zac and Zoe were by a shrub, Zac bent over, and Zoe was on her knees. Zoe's face was ashen, and she was holding something in her hands.

Double timing it down the slope went Dad and Mom, slipping and sliding around some, loose gravel spilling. As they closed in, they could see Zoe holding a gold chain necklace.

Holding his hand out, Zac demanded, "Lemme see it, c'mon I want to see it. Give it to me."

"No, I found it first."

"Let me see it, now!"

Zac started to grab at it, but Zoe had a tenacious grip on the necklace, "I'm holding it for now."

Perplexed, Mom ambled over, "What is going on?"

Rubbing his sandy hair, Dad asked, "Yes, why did you yell Zoe?"

Staring intently at them with her big green eyes. Zoe questioned, "What was the name of Governor Meyers daughter?"

Dad said, "I think… Alexandra."

"That's right," agreed Mom.

Cautiously Zoe asked; "Did she have a nickname?"

"I'm not sure what it was." Dad replied.

Thinking about it Zac snapped his fingers, "Wait a minute-- Alexi?"

Holding out the necklace like she was holding a snake, "I think it was Lexi. Look at the name on the necklace."

Standing up, Zoe presented it to her parents. It looked like a 14-carat gold necklace, with fine interwoven links, in the middle were the gold letters that said *Lexi*."

"Oh, my God!" exclaimed Mom.

Puzzled, Dad commented, "Could it be that's it's the necklace belonging to the governor's daughter, Alexandra Meyers?"

Examining the necklace closely, with Zoe breathing down Mom's neck. Mom said it sure could be from one of Governor Meyers children.

Crowing in Zac looked at it. "Then they need to be rescued. We need to rescue them. I'm thinking of kicking someone's butt."

"ZAC!" Mom's face was stern.

Raising his eyebrows. "Mom, I just said I was thinking of kicking some butt."

Zoe scolded Zac, "Way to go bro with you and your karate. You are going to get us trouble before we can even get out of the park."

The drive back to the Pine Motel seemed long, so did the kids arguing on the way make it seemed longer. They talked about the FBI agent, the necklace and of course what they were going to have for dinner tonight.

"Tonight, we can eat—PIZZA!" Zoe giggled.

Disagreeing like a brother, Zac said you always want pizza."

"But I'm thinking Mexican tonight." Said Mom.

"What word? Did you guys say?" Dad had a smirk on his face. "Did I hear somebody want Taco's."

The kids started chanting together, "Pizza, pizza, pizza…"

Mom tried chanting, "Taco, taco, taco."

Dad even tried to help along, "Taco—taco."

Persistently Zac and Zoe went on wearing down their parents.

Giving it one more chance Dad chanted Taco's.

But as you would have it, the kid's chanting won.

Next thing you knew was Mom on her cellphone ordering. …a large Ham and pineapple pizza, a medium four cheese pizza, and a large deluxe hand tossed, with extra black olives…"

Running over, Zac reminded her, "Don't forget to make the Hawaiian, half Ham, and half sausage."

"Okay that's right, make the Hawaiian half ham and half sausage."

 Pausing on the phone, Mom listened.

 "You can be here within the hour, that's great. We will be hungry by then, bye."

Zoe started getting out the Uno cards. "Let's play till the pizza arrives."

Complaining, Zac said, "An hour is a long time on an empty belly, Mom."

"Yah, Mother a long, long time." Even Steven was rubbing his belly.

Trying to console them, Mom said, "You all just need to wait, we will survive."

When you're young, an hour is a long time to wait with an empty stomach.

CHAPTER 4

The Lund's were playing cards with some limited arguing that was going on or calling it a family disagreement if you like. Zac won the first game, Zoe won the second game, halfway through the third game.

Down to one card loudly Dad said, "Uno." There was a knock on the motel door.

Lori said, "Father, get the door."

"But I'm down to one card. Have Zac get it."

"Make Dad get it." Zac said jokingly.

"No, you get it Zac." Giggled Zoe.

Having to say only one word. Mom commanded, "Door!"

Complaining, Dad got up, "Okay, okay! Pick up the cards, but I'm going to say I won this game."

Mom picked up the table, pronto. The food was paid for with plastic, the pizza cartons opened, and the first bites taken.

"Wait! Stop eating, it's time to pray." said Dad.

Taking another bite, Zac said chewing his food, "It's okay, I just had a test bite, Dad."

"Wait I need a test bite also." Quickly Zoe stuffed her mouth with a bite.

The Lund's prayed and the pizzas were consumed. The few remaining pieces were stuffed in one box and placed in the refrigerator for a mid-night snack. Zac grabbed his phone and sat on the edge of a bed. He pointed the phone at the TV and mirrored a newscast to the screen.

A young Asian man, his dark hair short and neat, started speaking. His brown eyes were about two shades lighter than his hair. They were clear and bright. "As of today, there is no report on Alexandra and Waldo Meyers's the Governors missing children. There is a reward for any information leading to the discovery of the children." A picture flashed of the two children, the girl tall, and slender, the boy short and stout. "A ransom demand has been made for an undisclosed amount, there have been…"

"Stop it right there and go back a bit." Zoe went over and stood in front of the two-meter TV screen.

Touching his phone, Zac rewound the footage.

"Right there, stop." With her glittered fingernail, Zoe pointed to the girl on the screen. "Look, Mom and Dad, right—here." As she talked, Zoe's voice became high and shrill. "It's the same necklace that I found, it says *Lexi.*"

Sure, enough on the screen around the young victim's neck dangled the image of the necklace Zoe had found. Zoe ran over to Dad; he gave her a reassuring hug. Mom went over to the dresser and picked up the necklace and held it against the screen. It was a perfect match.

Prying herself off Dad, Zoe stood by Mom. "Mom what are we going to do?"

Mom handed her the necklace, there was a tear in Zoe's eye. She held it up to her face and then looked at the screen. "The Meyers children will be okay, honey."

Dad took over, "First thing tomorrow, I will go to the Sheriff's office and report the necklace and the location of where we found it. I will also talk to my buddy rangers at Yosemite Park. Steven's voice deepened, "Don't worry honey, we will get to the bottom of this. The Meyers kids will be found!" Dad pounded his fist into his left palm.

Wack!

"Are you going to kick their butts, Dad? You are a 3rd degree black belt." Zac punched and kicked the air. He was about to test for his 1st degree black belt. "I'll help you."

"Me too now that I'm a blue belt." Zoe leaped and did a remarkably high double front kick. The two power kids started around the motel room, jumping up and down punching and kicking--but not for long.

"STOP! This is not a dojo, it's a motel room and other people can hear you stomping around. And if Dad is going to kick some people's butts, he might need to take Uncle Scott along." Mom had spoken.

Making a sour face, Dad said, "I don't need my brother, if there's three or less, I can take them."

Calmly Mom put her hand on her husband's broad shoulder, "Steven, they've already killed a trained F.B.I. agent… and if there are more than three? And what if they have guns? Need I say more."

Dad let out a deep sigh, "Okay, honey. You're right I got carried away with the excitement. Zac, we have had enough of the news. Let's microwave some popcorn and watch a movie."

Touching his phone screen, Zac asked, "What are we watching tonight, Dad?"

Dad pretended to think, "Everybody loves Jackie Chan movies, right?"

For once, the family all agreed. Dad grabbed his tablet; he tapped it a few times.

"Here it is. This is a new Charlie Chan movie. That's Jackie's number one son. It's his third movie."

"What's the title?" asked Mom, who took over and started watching the first bag of popcorn pop. The Lund's might go through four or five bags.

"Zoe, please get out the Parmesan cheese out and don't forget the Garlic salt."

"Okay, Mom. I'm on it."

"They are continuing the 'Rush Hour' series. Charlie Chan is in it and believe it or not, Chris Tucker's son is in it too. They call it The Rush Hour Sons."

Zac frowned, "You're making that up, Dad."

"Busted." Dad chuckled, "It's actually Rush Hour 7. But I thought my name sounded much funnier."

Zac and Zoe gave each other the look about Dad being corny.

Eating the popcorn, the family watched and enjoyed the movie. It was funny, cheesy, and silly, but as most sequels go, not as good as the original three movies. Although the movie had been quite thrilling with a hilarious firetruck chase scene at the end of the movie. They ate popcorn like it was going out of style and they laughed and laughed. But it might be the last laugh the Lund's will have for a while, for the Governor's kids' lives were on the line.

Tomorrow would be quite a different day.

Day 3

The Grizzly Giant, at the Mariposa grove at Yosemite. One of the most photographed trees in the world. The tree is quite a sight to see, in fact photos don't do the tree justice.

Having to ask Zoe said, "Do I look cute?"

And Zoe did look cute, the sun filtering through the trees making her curly strawberry blonde hair dance and her green eyes sparkle. Standing in front of the Grizzly Giant sequoia tree Zoe was making a heart shape with her hands. She looked quite petite in front of the 65-meter towering tree. Mother Lori had her SONY 10K camera ready for action. Poses were performed and pictures were taken, this went on for quite a while.

Bored out of his skull for Zac, a short eternity seemed to be going by, "Are you two done yet? It there any angle you two haven't thought of yet."

"Hang on there, Zac." Mom moved about for one more different pose.

"Agreeing with Mom, "Hold your horses Zac."

Bored Zac looked at his phone, "Do you know this tree is the second tallest tree in the park and the 26th largest tree in the world? They estimate the sequoia is over 2,000 years old."

"Take another one, Mom." Zoe yelled.

"Okay, but this is the last one. We don't want to keep brother waiting."

Holding his hands up in the air, Zac smiled.

"He can wait for me."

"Zoe."

This time she had climbed partway up a half a meter of the thick rugged bark, Zoe stuck out her left arm and was waving. Zac snuck a peek at her, he wouldn't admit it, but she was kinda pretty and cute— for a sister. He went back to his phone; a low whistle escaped his lips.

"What now, Zac?" asked Mom.

"I'm studying up on this crazy tree, Mom. It weighs over 2 million pounds, that's like stacking 150 elephants on top of each other and some of the branches are two meters thick. How can something organic get so big and massive?"

Lowering the camera, Mom went over to Zac, they scrolled through some pictures together and info about the majestic trees. "How does that work Zac?"

"The trick is to keep the trees growing and protect forest health and reduce the risk of fire danger. Draught is another factor."

"Isn't there some sort of beetles that attack the trees also?"

"Yes, Mom there is a bark beetle as a newly observed cause of death. Hey Zoe, come look at these photos... Zoe? Zoe!"

No answer, in fact Mom and Zac turned to the Grizzly Giant. There was no Zoe.

Calling out loudly at the top of his lungs, "ZOE! Zoe, where the heck are you?"

Mom frowned; she used the Mom voice, "Zoe come on out—now!"

Zac stalked over to the tree, "Yea sis, get out here now. We know your hiding." Zac put a finger to his mouth and then pointed to the other side of the mammoth tree.

Getting the hint, Lori jogged to the far side of the Grizzly and stopped. They nodded to each other and snickered some. Nodding, the two Lund's blasted in different directions around to the back of the tree trunk. Together they yelled. "Surprise!"

There was no one there to surprise.

There was a moment of panic. Lori screamed at the top of lungs, "Zooooooeeeeee!"

Zac ran another lap around the giant tree, it took him a moment. "She's not here Mom, where is she? Did she get kidnapped?"

"Bite your tongue Zac, don't you dare say that. She's hiding and playing a trick on us."

"I'll check on her Mom."

In frustration Zac ran another lap around the tree and made it back to Mom. Zac was panting by now. "Mom, she's gone, I know she's a brat sometimes, but she wouldn't run away."

Seeing the look of concern on the young man's face, Mom kept her face blank. "I'm sure she's around here, she must have seen something, got distracted, and wandered off."

Between deep breaths, Zac said, "I sure hope so. Do we go look for her or stay here and hope she comes back?"

"Hang on Zac, let's think about this for a moment."

"Boy is Dad going to be mad about this."

"I'm not going to lose a child Zac. Calm down."

Trying to be funny, Zac said, "You haven't lost one yet."

Ignoring him, Mom kept scanning the park, worry on her face.

"Here I am everybody and look what I found."

Mom and Zac spun around, walking out of the bushes stood Zoe. Zac about had to change his pants, Zoe stood there holding a—bear cub! The bear

47

looked small, furry, and cute with shades of brown and tan; maybe it weighed 5 kilograms. Zoe held it in her arms, surprisingly it did not fight to get out of Zoe's arms. It sat there snuggling and licking at her cheek, much like a puppy dog.

Quickly, Zac and Mom strode to Zoe with her squirming prize package. Mom held out her hand, the bear sniffed and licked her forefinger.

"How old is he, Mom?" asked Zoe. I found his head stuck in a log and I pulled him out. Can I keep him?"

Mom's green eyes got bigger, she shook her head and said one word, "No."

"Just kidding about keeping him, Mom. I know better, but the look on your face looked priceless."

Zac actually laughed out loud at Zoe's comment. As the big brother, he rarely laughed at her jokes.

"That's a good one Zoe."

Rubbing the cub's fur behind its ears. Mom stated, "It can't be three months old at best. You say it got stuck?"

Zoe's face got serious, "Mom, I know better. Since you're a veterinarian, I should know better than to pick one up. He needed rescuing; I saved his hide so to speak. We can take him and feed him food."

Speaking up, Zac said, "I thought they only drank mother's milk at that age."

Mom agreed, "You're correct Zac, so he must have been curious and poked his head in the fallen trunk and got stuck. Good job on the rescue Zoe, but we're going to be in a big mess when momma bear comes looking."

Zac started to speak, but as if on cue a roar was heard from the woods. It was not a good thing. It sent chills down the backs of the Lund's. A second roar sounded out this time it seemed louder and closer.

With a trembling voice, Zoe asked, "What do I do Mom?"

Mom directed, "Race to the back of the tree and put down the cub, pronto."

Zac called out, "Here sis, let's go—now!"

Before she could answer, Zac Grabbed Zoe's hand. Zac yanked hard as they headed to the back of the enormous tree. Having no choice Zoe followed and Mom raced to her backpack at the same time. A third roar permeated the woods, it was way too close for comfort. Zoe deposited the bear cub and gave it a final caress. It's paw tapped her hand, like a high five. Then the kids raced back around the tree to Mom and stood by her side. The bad news is the cub loped along following Zoe.

"Go away bear." Zoe begged, "Get out of here, go away. Go back to Momma. Shoo!"

As you can guess, the bear cub went for Zoe like she was magnetized. Zoe waved frantically at the cub to leave.

Zoe voice high and shrill with fear. "Get out of here. Now! Go back to Momma. Go!"

Plopping back down, the cub innocently sat on its haunches and gave a stare at Zoe.

Waving at the cub like brushing away a fly, Zoe yelled, "Go now!"

No reaction, the little black bear just sat there.

"Go get!" Yelled Zac trying to help.

Yelling again, "Go home bear. Go to your momma. Zoe folded her hands together prayer like."

Bending over, Mom started rummaging about in her backpack. Zoe went and stood behind her brother, in a crouched position. Picking up a thick one-meter stick, Zac hefted it in his right hand. Around the tree Momma, the black bear appeared. She looked huge, frightening, and mad! Drool and foam dripped from the bear's mouth as she growled.

The cub started to wander around like it didn't have a care in world, but Momma bear cared, and she cared plenty. Momma reared up on her hind legs, all three meters of her. She was a titan, and she was ticked off. The black bear roared again; so close that you could smell her foul breath. Lori popped up from her backpack, rutting through it like her life depend on it and it probably did. Now Lori held out a cannister the size of an aerosol spray can. The bear dropped to all four growled and charged at the Lund's! The bear's mouth frothy, it's fangs yellow, and it's beady eyes blood red. Momma bear was intent on death and destruction!

Chapter 5

Banding the stick about it looked like Zac was going to swat a fly, which the bear definitely wasn't. He stood his ground, a brave young man. Momma bear's feet on the move, but Momma Lund was also on the move . Lori charged over in front of her two children, came to an abrupt stop and she whirled facing the jaws of death. The sudden movement of Lori surprised Momma Bear, she paused just for a second. A second being all Momma Lund needed, she pointed the cannister at the bear which was only a few meters away and pushed down on the nozzle.

A cloud of 2% oleoresin capsicum filled a four-meter area. Aggressively Lori waved her hand about and sustained spraying. Lori surged forward discharging the container of pepper spray forcing the bear backward. Roaring in displeasure, the bear went crazy with its eyes, nose and skin inflamed from the discharge. The bear reared upward trying to avoid the pepper spray. It made a hideous sneeze, snot running from its nose, turned its tail and tried rubbing its nose repeatedly in the grass and weeds, but to no avail. It's groans, cries, and moans were pitiful.

The baby bear cub ran over to its mother, shifting its' position, it pawed the ground and whined. After circling her Momma, the bear cub then ran off and Momma bear reluctantly chased after her cub. Momma stopped at the edge of the trees, growled, and made a moan of fear that scared bears do as danger passes. Then they were gone, but the memories would haunt the Lund's for years.

Dropping the spent cannister of Sabre Red Pepper, Lori hugged Zac and Zoe. The three embraced emphatically. Danger had passed, at least for the moment. The Lund's seldom had dull moments, that's for sure.

Through tears in her eyes Zoe said, "Wow! Zac you were protecting me and only with a stick."

Zac claimed, "Actually, I was protecting Mom."

Zoe didn't buy it, "Thanks anyway you big goof."

Mumbling, Zac said, "Your welcome."

Earlier that day, Steven got out on the passenger side of the Cherokee and walked around to the driver's window. The tinted window rolled down.

"Goodbye, Lori." He gave his wife a brief kiss on the lips. "You three have fun on your hike and check out that Grizzly Bear tree." After hearing the bear incident Dad said, "Hopefully that's the only bear you will see today."

"Goodbye husband."

"Bye, Dad." Zac adding, "Have a great day."

"Yeah we will miss you Dad." Zoe waved goodbye.

Poking his head back into the vehicle, Steven gave them the "Dad" look. "And listen up kids, no fighting or arguing, remember we're on vacation. Remember by making Mom happy that way we are all happy."

Giving a loving smile, Lori blew Steven a kiss, "LYB." (Love you by)

About face, Steven walked across the parking lot. He entered the Sherrif's office, just a small remote office just outside the park. Since it was so small it had no dispatcher, and usually only one officer remained on duty. The deputy on duty today happened to be the same one the Lund's had met at Yosemite Park. The gold badge read, Williams. He got out of his chair, greeted Steven, and shook his hand.

"Lund, correct?"

"That's right and you're Deputy Williams?"

"Troy Williams and I want to apologize for the other day for the way I acted." He cleared his throat, "I mean what are the odds of your kids finding a dead body in the park? Then I heard the news about the F.B.I. agent. It was shocking news, about the Governor's children missing. There is an APB out for them and a manhunt going on. We're on overload here.

Calmly Steven stated, "Noted. It is quite the predicament."

Troy asked formally, "What can I do for you, Ranger Lund?"

Looking down, Steven had forgotten he had his park outfit on, green pants, gray shirt, and arrowhead emblem on his left sleeve. "It's about a necklace."

"A necklace?" echoed Deputy Williams.

"My daughter found a gold chain necklace in the park that is most likely Governor Meyers' daughter's necklace. It says *Lexi* on it."

Lines appeared on Troy's tanned forehead, "You found the Meyers's girl necklace. We need to report this! You still have possession of it?"

"Yes, Zoe found it, and of course we still have possession. I came to report the location of where it was found."

Troy rubbed his hands together in excitement, "That's great news, now we start a new search grid."

I can give the exact location, It's saved on my Garmin GPS."

"Brillant, that's using your head Lund."

"I'm just using common sense."

The door opened, a gust of wind blew in and with it a short man in a Park Ranger outfit. The man entered and took off his hat, he nodded to the Deputy and looked at Steven. A broad smile of recognition broke out on his face.

"Steven, it's so good to see you."

"Joe, Joe Hartley, it's good to see you too."

The men did a half bro hug and pulled apart.

"What can I do for you, Hartley?"

"You know me Williams, I'm always around working and hanging out at the park. Today I came by to meet my old buddy, Steven Lund. I'm here to take him to our ANPR Convention."

"What's that?" asked Troy.

Steven explained, "It's for the Association of National Park Rangers. That's part of the reason I'm here and to get a deduction for some of my family vacation travel expenses."

Smiling tightly, Joe said, "Steven's always thinking, and he is usually way ahead of the game. I've known him and his brother Scott for maybe six or seven years."

"Probably closer to eight years I'm thinking," mused Steven. "I remember we met when we busted the illegal fur trappers in Custer State park in the Black Hills."

"Yeah, that was sick. Tough job, yet somehow rewarding after it was done." Joe rubbed his left shoulder.

Steven recalled, "That's right, you got shot in the shoulder as a reward for your efforts. I had to half carry you to the first aid station. That was an ordeal."

"It was just a scratch Steven, I've had worse."

"Have you now, you…"

Troy interrupted them, "Hold on guys for a moment before you two swap stories. I want to know more about this necklace that your daughter found."

"Necklace?" asked Joe.

Steven answered, "Yes, it the Governor's daughter, Alexandra's necklace."

Joe's eyes got bigger. "That's big news, Governor Meyers daughter and son have been kidnapped."

Sadly, Troy shook his head, "We know that Joe, we need to find those kids. Our searching so far has been unproductive. Not a clue so far."

Steven added, "And as a father they need to be found ASAP. I'm sure their parents are worried sick. Hopefully the necklace will give us a led." Steven reached into his shirt pocket and produced the shiny silver necklace, with the small letters, *LEXI*. He handed it to Troy for inspection.

Troy snatched it, perhaps too fast. He caught himself and said, "Thanks." He set the necklace on his desk, picked up a GoPro action camera and promptly took a couple photos. Like a man on a mission, Troy went to the desk top computer and started downloading the pictures. Troy turned back to the men, "This might just be the break we needed."

"That's quite the find, Steven." Said Joe.

"I didn't find it, my daughter Zoe did in the park." Steven explained what Zac and Zoe did to Joe and Troy.

"Wait, what were the coordinates Lund?" Troy sat ready to type on his computer.

Steven held out the Garmin and read them off.

"That will be I great help, or at least I hope so." Troy said eagerly, and started to type them in.

Looking at his Amazfit Bip 8 watch, Joe said, "We better get going or we're going to be late."

"Don't worry, Ranger's I'm on it and will keep you updated on the progress. Tell your daughter…" Troy's face went blank.

"Zoe."

"Tell Zoe she did a great job, and she can sleep good tonight. Thanks."

Steven nodded, "Yes, keep us posted."

Joe said, "Good luck."

"Don't worry I will let you know what's going on."

The two Park Ranger's left, and the deputy went to work on the computer.

Zac had been lecturing Zoe for whatever good it would do, "…trying to rescue that bear cub was just plain stupid Zoe, you almost got us in big trouble. Don't ever do that again."

"I tell you he was stuck. We both know better, Mom has trained us well being an exotic animal veterinarian. But the little guy needed help, and we are trained to help people and animals."

Shaking his head vehemently, "What you did was wrong! The bear cub was wild, he would have somehow found his way out or his mother would have rescued him."

Zoe's voice was shrill by now. "But I had to rescue him, I couldn't leave me alone. You being a pest Zac, just stop."

Zac had trouble keeping his mouth shut, as kids often do. So, he said, "Thank God Mom's about as tough as Dad, her charging in with that bear spray saved the day. It saved your bacon."

"Don't call me bacon, Zac. Just shut up."

"But I thought everybody liked bacon."

"Just stupid boys like you."

"Zoe just called me stupid."

"Zac you always complain when I call you stupid."

"Stupid is stupid."

"I called boys stupid, not Zac even though he may be."

"It's the same thing Zoe and you're the one that's stupid."

"I am not stupid."

"What about the bear cub? That was stupid thing to do."

"He needed rescuing. Somebody had to help him. I couldn't leave him all alone. He was so cute and needed help."

"Zoe you need to think better about things like that in the future. If there is trouble come get me, Mom or Dad."

"Okay Zac maybe I will."

Still mad about the event, Zac went on. "This is serious you could have got us all killed or at least maimed by the Momma bear. You need to quit pulling your crazy stunts."

Upset, Zoe defended herself, "The cub was stuck, he could have died in the tree trunk. He need my help. Stop picking on me."

But Zac didn't stop talking.

While the two youths were arguing a dark blue Ford E-transit Cargo Van pulled into the Motel parking lot and parked. Two men dressed in dark got out of the vehicle, one opened the rear door, and it looked like he got out some bags of groceries. Zac hushed them, they had been taught not to argue in public especially with stranger's present and the two men definitely looked like strangers. But Zoe kept talking anyway.

"Tell me the truth Zac, I know you act all tough and that, but wouldn't you have tried to rescue the bear cub? You love dogs and animals, right?"

The question remained unanswered as Zac and Zoe's attention was diverted. One of the two men went to open a motel room door, the other man pushed a button, and the rear tail gate slid upward. He got out a bag of clothes, they seemed to be children's clothes. Zac and Zoe stood still, they could not help but watch. The other man got out plastic bags of food, two handfuls.

Zac thought, *That's a lot to eat for only two men.*

The bags were full of crackers, chips, candy, juices, and stuff for snacks.

"What is going on here?

To Zoe , Zac said, "Let's keep this between us and monitor them."

His sister got excited, "You mean like spy on them?"

Zac's arched his eyebrow; "Sure, let's go with that."

"You're on bro, I'm a good spy. We could be the Spykids."

"Okay whatever, sis. But let's get to our room so Mom and Dad don't worry about us. C'mon Zoe, besides after looking at all that food I'm hungry for pizza and popcorn and whatever movie Dad has planned for us tonight."

Agreeing, "I getting hungry too. I don't know how Dad does it, but he always has the best movies for us. Lets' head back and get a snack to hold us over."

Mumbling something, Zac agreed.

Okay bro, let's go."

"In just a moment, Sis."

As Zac eyed the room the two men had entered and memorized the room number. Tonight, would be fun for the Lund's, but in the back of everyone's mind they all were worried thinking of the whereabouts and misfortune of Meyer's two children. Poor Alexi and Waldo, and their parents. What kind of night, a night of misery for the entire family to be sure.

CHAPTER 6

DAY 4

There was rain and then there is rain, but this night the rain was torrential. It seemed as if the floodgates of heaven had opened up. The thunderstorms started about 1:00 am, the crack and boom of the thunder had woken up the entire Lund family. The vibrations threatened to shatter the windows of the motel room, or so it seemed. The family had hardly been asleep for more than an hour or so, they had stayed up and had fun watching a movie.

A brilliant flash of lightning showed through the cracks of the curtains, a few seconds later the thunder had started.

KA-BOOM!

The windows rattled, the sky was accentuated by the zagged lightning bolts. Everybody was grouchy and tired after such a short sleep, but the storm was just warming up. Multiple flashes of light lit up the room, it was like a strobe light going off and on. A series of loud bangs, the snaps of thunder were not only heard they were felt. The echoes of the booms followed, the windows and beds vibrated from the thunderclaps. An awful sound commenced; it was the roar of trainlike sounds.

Mumbled sleepily, Zac commented, "That one made my teeth rattle. I just want to go back to sleep."

A half-awake Zoe half sat up, she rubbered her eyes like she could take away the tiredness, "When will it stop? I'm so tired. It needs to stop. That last thunderclap was a lulu."

"Zoe you know that you can't turn off a storm." Inside Zac was tired but he wouldn't show it.

"Dad—can you check the window?" Asked Zoe.

Prying Lori's arm off him, Steven managed to climb out of bed. "Okay, Okay, let me check." He went to the window and drew back the curtain. The parking lot looked beyond wild, rain drops pelting the cars, the rain striking so hard the drops were ricocheting off the hoods and tops of the vehicles.

"It's a Mother of a Storm." He called back.

Suddenly, Zac was standing next to Dad, "You're not kidding, it's sick out there."

Lifting his cellphone, Steven's finger tapped the weather app. The screen showed green, with lots of patches of yellow and red highlights. "Sorry gang, this is just the beginning of a monster storm. They are already calling for flash flood alerts, this will go on all night and well into the morning."

The high voice called out, "Dad, I know I'm a big girl, but a daughter can snuggle with her father—right?"

Tilting Dad's head, "Yes, you're never too old to snuggle Zoe, Mom and I still do it." Steven looked in wonderment at his wife, Lori, still lay asleep on the bed, like a *Sleeping Beauty*.

"Zoe, go get your tablet and we'll put on a show and watch it in bed."

Needing to lay down, Dad gave a farewell glance at the raging powerful storm. To emphasize the point, more lightning flashed, splitting the dark clouds into fragments, like pieces of a puzzle falling apart. He pulled the curtains closed to minimize the lightning, but the booming thunder could not be stopped. Walking over Dad laid down on top of the bed covers next to Zoe who was pulling up an anime movie about Emoji's.

Leaning against Dad's shoulder, Zoe gave out a huge yawn. A mighty BOOM sounded, shaking the bed, Zoe pressed tighter to Dad. A minute later a mute Zac, with a pillow crawled into the other side of the bed and laid down. Dad looked at Zac, they both nodded at each other and then watched the movie. Dad smiled, he was always happiest when he was sandwiched by Zac and Zoe. Steven knew he did not have many years or even months till the kids would think they were too big to snuggle, but he was going to get all the time he could get away with. About an hour later, the three of them fell asleep. The angry storm continued unabated and unnoticed by the Lund family.

Nothing like an irritating alarm going off after a rough night of semi-sleep. Dad's bleary eyes opened they were more red than amber brown, he managed to look at his phone it was 7:04. He sighed and shrugged his broad shoulders, he had to get up and go to the ranger station for more meetings. He hoped to be done by noon and skate out to spend time with his family. As he started to get up, Zac's right eye popped open, you couldn't get by anything with Zac, him being a light sleeper like his dad and Uncle Scott.

"Time to get up Dad?"

"Not for you go back to sleep son."

"Okay—but I get up if you need me."

"Thanks but you can stay in bed. I'm going to work."

"I'm awake." But Zac rolled over anyway, perhaps falling asleep.

Dad also rolled over on his side, half asleep and half awake. He more slid or sort fell out of bed and the sheets, to the carpeted floor on his knees, then got up. Dad went over, fumbled around in the closet, and got dressed in his park ranger outfit as quietly as possible. Zac opened the other eye and climbed out of bed, got a bottle of water. Sitting on a chair, Steven put his boots on. Got up and looked in the mirror at his dark blondish hair, ratted and messy from the bad night's sleep,

Sitting in a chair, Zac tried to force a smile at Dad, but a look of exhaustion crossed his face instead. Going over and used his hand to playfully, Dad messed up Zac's hair even more. Which normally would annoy Zac, but he was too tired to care at the moment.

A trip to the minifridge needed to happen, Dad got a bottle of water and texted a messaged on his cellphone. Zac picked up his tablet, and the two Lund's sat in silence for the moment. Getting up, Dad went to the bathroom. A few minutes later he returned, then Dad went over to Zoe, pushed aside a pair of cute curls and lightly kissed Zoe on her forehead. Kids are so cute when they are asleep. He walked over and hovered over his wife, Lori, she looked about as cute as Zoe. He bent over to give her a goodbye kiss on her forehead.

Suddenly, a hand grasped his wrist in a vise like grip. "Oh no you don't mister; you're not sneaking out of here. I can get cleaned up, dressed, and take you to your meeting."

Inside, Steven knew that Lori would be about an hour before he could leave, Lori was never fast about getting ready. So, Dad planted a kiss on Mom's lips.

SMACK!

Somewhat, Mom reciprocated. Their lips touched kissing twice more, and if your under 12 years old-- Eck!

"I need to get going honey, the meeting won't wait."

"I said I would drive you. I'll can get ready fast."

"But…but Lori."

"It's okay honey, I got a great night of sleep. I'm ready to roll."

Shaking his head in disbelief, "I'm glad somebody had a great night of sleep."

"Wait a minute when I woke up... "Lori licked her dry lips, "Did you sleep with one of the kids?"

"Yea, the three of us sort of hung out."

"What? Did you have a bad night of sleep, husband?"

"Lori you could sleep through tornado, in fact you practically did."

She wrinkled her forehead, "Did it storm last night?"

"Something like that, how about Joe Hartley picks me up and takes me to the meeting? I already texted him and he can drive over here and get me. That way you guys can keep the Jeep and get around till I get out, which should be about lunch time."

Thinking about it, "It's no big deal to drive you in, Zac's almost 16, he can stay with Zoe for the short time it takes me to drive you. We can spend some time together away from the kids and talk. I'll clean up super-fast."

Talk, Lori wanted to talk, women always want to talk. Steven wanted time to think before the meeting— not talk. How could he get out of it? "Are you sure it's okay to leave the kids?"

"They have martial art training; Zac has a cellphone and we're in a public motel."

"But honey…"

Lori folded her arms. Steven knew he couldn't out argue anything, with Lori's stubbornness.

She continued, "To be honest honey, I love our kids, but I need a break even if it's for an hour. We'll sneak out, get coffee, and drop you off. Also, that way I can say hello to the people at the meeting."

Letting out a deep breath, Steven knew that Lori was a social butterfly, she not only loved being a veterinarian and working with animals, but she loved people too. Frequently, she was on FB and IG.

"So, what can I say honey? Whatever floats your boat, it's always hard to say no to you. Let's go. I'll talk to the kids while you get ready."

Smiling Lori said, "You're a dear, I get ready in warp speed."

Dad's reward came with another kiss. Lori then scampered to the bathroom to get ready, grabbing clothes as she went.

Shaking his head, Dad went to wake up Zoe and Zac. "Rise and shine!"

Slowly Zoe rose and Zac crawled out of bed, they argued for a moment as they were waking up. Zoe stretched and reluctantly complained to Dad about having to wake up. Zac also protested about being tired and not getting enough sleep.

Mom's voice cracked the air like a whip, from out of the bathroom door. "Get dressed--now. We need to get going or Dad will be late."

The kids still wanted to argued, perhaps a bit less.

Dad's deep voice boomed, but not quite as loud as last night's thunder. "Mom's right, we need to leave soon. Can we trust you two?"

Agreeing Zac said, "Yes."

Elbowing his sister, "Say yes."

"Dad, Zac just hit me."

"I did not."

Dad questioned Zac, "Did you hit her?"

"Not really, I did not hit her, it was just a small poke. She's making things up." Zac turned to Zoe, "Quit lying."

Zoe voice became high pitch and loud. "I did not lie, you're the lair."

"I am not lying, I just touched you." Zac declared.

Having to level with them, Dad said, "You two need to quit calling each other liars, whether someone lies or not. Listen up, Zac and Zoe telling a lie doesn't make you a liar. If you guys don't calm down and behave you can both come with us—and with no devices."

For a rare moment the room became silent. Zad and Zoe looked at each other, then smiles began to form, then came the laughter and giggling. Dad resisted laughing with them, trying hard to keep a straight face.

Coming into the room, messing with her hair, Mom frowned. "What going on?"

Explaining to his wife, "I was just testing those two to see if they wanted to come with."

At the same time Zac and Zoe said, "Can't we stay, we will behave."

"Yeah Dad, we'll be fine. Zoe and I can get along."

Zoe gave her signature pouty lower lip, it was somewhere between cute and pathetic. Dad had a hard time resisting her. "Can't I stay here Dad? I promise that I will behave."

"Me too Dad. We will be fine." Zac gave his best solum look.

Catching on quickly, Mom teased, "I'm sure they can't spend enough time in our Jeep. Let's take them with us."

The look on the kid's faces went blank, "What?"

Dad said nothing, which was smart.

Mom clapped her hands, once. "All right kids, you all know the rules while we're gone, right?"

Zoe instantly responded, "Yes Mom, no fighting or arguing."

"And don't answer the door and don't order Door Dash either—right? Dad said.

"What if I get really hungry." Zac rubbed his stomach unconvincingly. "Just a bite?"

Lori wasn't going to argue, "No Door Dash, that's final, eat one of our power bars and have a juice pouch, then text me what you want for breakfast.

We're on vacation, I'll get whatever you guys want and bring it back."

"Whatever I want?!?" Zac's mind saw a swirl of food swimming around in his head. "C'mon sis, let's go online and look at some menu's."

"That sounds like a plan." Zoe giggled. "Bye Mom and Dad don't let the door hit you on the way out."

Dad said, "You two better do a lot of hiking this afternoon, to burn off the carbs. But first, Zac can you check on the Flash flooding after last night's monsoon and when you go hiking check for a safe area. They will be listed on the Yosemite website."

Dancing over, Zoe stood on her tiptoes, and gave Dad a peck on his cheek, Mom got a brief hug.

"Bye guys." Zac waved bye while sipping juice, he went to his tablet to shop for food.

The Lund's walked out to the Jeep, they embraced for a long moment.

"Okay Lori, you got what you wanted. Let's grab a breakfast sandwich and hash brown on the way."

As they disengaged, Lori said, "And don't forget the coffee."

"That's no problem after the bad night of sleep I got, I might even get two coffees." Steven smiled, "And I know just the place, theirs a terrific little diner on the way that has carry out."

"Okay honey." Lori smiled back. "Let's get going, you know how much food Zac can eat. The longer I'm gone the hungrier he'll get."

70

Steven rumbled in a gruff voice, "Quick, to the Batmobile!"

CHAPTER 7

Lori's response was instant, "I'm on it."

Suddenly he two Lund's were standing outside by the Jeep

Quickly, Lori got in, Steven jumped into the passenger side, and they seat belted up. Starting the engine, Lori slammed it into reverse, the tire's chirped, burned rubber and kicked up gravel.

"Wow! Honey we're not in that big a hurry. I won't be late." The family all knew that Lori was the hotrod of the group.

"Okay Steven, it's no big deal. A girl has to have some fun."

Leaning back into the leather seat, Steven commented, "Yeah, yeah. Let's take it easy, we're on vacation."

"Well lets have some fun. Off we go!"

That ride back to the Motel would to be the last easy thing to happen to the Lund's on this vacation. From now on nothing would be to be easy from here on out.

Leaning forward looking out the motel window, Zoe watched her parent's drive away. She gave a wave goodbye that went unnoticed. Looking at the parked vehicles and the large puddles of standing water from last night's storm, she noticed the dark

Ford van parked nearby. As she scanned the parking lot for activity Zoe spied one of the mysterious men leaving a motel room. He had a bundle under his left arm, as he stepped off the curb his booted foot slipped on a puddle. The man stumbled but regained his balance. The bundle hit the pavement and partially split open. Hurriedly the man bent over retrieving the contents. The content being clothes. The clothes looked to small to belong to the man that had been carrying the bundle

Zoe's bright green eyes got big, bigger…and bigger. She stared at the clothes in disbelief, they were the clothes of teenagers, probably for a boy and a girl. What are adult men doing with youth clothes? That was a great question.

In a whirl Zoe spun around, "Zac, come quick!"

"What? Leave me alone. I'm checking out items that we can eat, I can probably get away with anything I want to eat. We eat so healthily at home, I want some junk food."

"I'm serious bro, something is going on outside. Remember those mysterious men last night? One of them dropped a bag of clothes in the parking lot."

Bothered by being interrupted, Zac said, "Shut up! So what? What's the big deal about a bag of clothes? Quit annoying me, food's more important now."

Anxious, Zoe stamped her foot, "Don't tell me to shut up. Listen to me Zac—they are kid's clothes. Pull up some pictures of Governor Meyer's children that are kidnapped, what were their names? Lexi and Waldorf?

Unglued his face from his tablet, Zac corrected her, "You mean Lexi and Waldo? What about them?"

"Just Google them now!...I mean please." Zoe checked out the window, the clothes were almost totally picked up by now. The other man was helping too. She now frantic at this point, "Hurry up!"

"Okay, okay, just give me a moment." Zac scrolled through a couple news feeds, he saw warnings and pictures of flash flooding of a river and local creeks. "Here you go sis, a picture of the missing Meyer kids."

"Give it to me."

Before he could start to hand the tablet to Zoe, but Zoe ripped it out of his hands. "Zoe! Don't yank it from me."

Ignoring his comment, Zoe looked at the picture. Some of the clothes in the picture looked similar or comparable to the messy clothes that fell out of the bag. She held up the tablet to the window, but the clothes were picked up. She frowned. "Zac those two men out there are the kidnappers. They have to be."

"What are you talking about? What kidnappers?"

"Do I have to spell it out to you? Come to the window quick."

"Okay—okay."

Shaking his head, Zac did get up and went to the window. Just as the last couple pieces of clothing was stuffed into a green plastic bag. The other man had brought a couple of garbage bags from their room. Zac had to wonder, could Zoe be right? They were kid's clothes. The men dressed in dark pants, and hoody's glanced around nervously, which did make them even suspicious to Zac. One of the men got into the driver's side of the Cargo Van and it looked like they were preparing to leave. What could Zac do? There wasn't time to call the police or the Sheriff's office. This could be a vital lead to finding the missing children.

"I don't know for sure, but Zoe, you might be right. Maybe they are the kidnapper's."

"I told you so, bro. They even look like bad guy's. Let's follow them."

"You want us to follow them?"

"Exactly, now get going."

"What are you thinking Zoe? Follow them and do what?

"We will figure it out as we go."

The gears in Zac's head were turning, he was about to ask Zoe what bad guys look like, but he didn't bother. Instead, he thought about following them. What a crazy idea, follow them?

As if Zoe read his mind, "Zac we need to follow them, there is no time to call the police."

The other man had started packing the E-Ford.

"Zoe, I can't drive for another year or so and even if I could, Mom took the Jeep. What are we going to do? And how can we be positive they are the kidnappers."

Rubbing her chin, Zoe's mind also was on overdrive. "We do need to follow them; I sense they are the bad guys. We need to rescue the kids, it hurts me when people suffer, and the Meyer's family is suffering big time."

"In this case for once I'm going to agree with you." He went to the chair and slouched down, Zac's forefinger tapped on the side of the tablet. "What are we going to do...what we going to do?"

Zoe's voice became frantic, "They are both in the van now, think fast brother."

Then at the same time the young Lund's said, "THE VAN!

Zac was halfway hoping that Zoe would disagree, she loved action and adventure. He stared at her, she seemed ready and willing. Zac won't say it to her face, but he knew he had a brave sister.

"Zac, we can climb in the back of the van."

"And then what?" Zac asked puzzled.

"We will...we will..."

"What, sis?"

Unfortunately, Zac had a point, what would they do?

"Slapping his hands together like he just swatted a fly. "I got is Sis. When we get to the place where the Meyer's kids are we call for help on my cellphone."

"Okay, you just do that."

"Why do you sound so down?"

"I wish I had my own cellphone." wined Zoe. She slapped her hands together loudly, "I'll get the backpack and my jacket. You go get your stuff. Let's go."

Zac still doubted the idea. "Seriously sis, you want us to climb into the back of the van." But Zac nevertheless found himself getting to his feet, getting his phone, a jacket, and a pocketknife as he raced to the motel door.

"What about a note for Mom and Dad?"

Zac shook his head, "No time, I'll text them when we're in the van."

"Okay, but I still think we should leave a note."

Big brother looked out the window, "We got to go, I'll handle it."

Zac and Zoe opened the door, and Zac paused for a moment.

Putting his hand on his sister's shoulder, "Remember to go slow, act naturally."

Putting her head up, "I know how to act."

"Yeah right."

They tried to walk outside casually through the parking lot and passed by the van like they were heading to the woods on the other side. Their steps were uneven and broken, ice raced about in their veins, and their two hearts were pounding rapidly.

77

Suddenly, as if they were one, they darted behind the van and stopped. Zoe threw a look at Zac, then at the van door daring Zac to open the door. Inside Zac was afraid, terribly afraid, fear raced up his spine, it numbed his brain but...

Zac needed courage, he recalled Uncle Scott and Dad talking once about hero's, not superheroes, but real people. Being a hero doesn't mean you're always brave, it means that you overcome your fear and do what you have to do. Today Zac and Zoe would be heroes. They would become the heroes that had come to save the day. Zac opened the door. They crawled into a dark scary place, the cargo hold of the van. No sooner than Zac had closed the door the van started backing up.

Readers put on your seatbelt for the exciting climax of **Mystery Among the Trees.** Hope for a happy ending for Zac and Zoe Lund. In today's world you just never know.

The ride seemed to take forever, an hour that seemed like a year to young people without patience. Each bump and rut seemed more of a mental torment than a physical discomfort. Zac had tried to text a message, but between the bumps and his nervous fingers he quickly abandoned the idea. He would text later when the E-van slowed down or stopped. The darkness inside pulled, tugged, and nagged on their minds, and their imagination and fear grew at each bump and rut in the road. The darkness seemed to solidify itself into creepy and crawling tentacles causing their skin to prickle and tingle.

Desperately Zoe reached out and grasped Zac's hand, Zac did not resist her as he normally would have. They clinched their hands together and hung on for dear life. When would this wild ride end? Then it got unexpectedly worse, the van stopped—silence. Zac and Zoe's ears perked up as they heard the click of two doors opening, a pause…and then a deep clunk, clunk of the two door's closing. Zac wondered, would they open the rear cargo doors?"

Zac dared to turn on the flashlight, in the illumination Zoe's face appeared as white as a ghost. Zac wanted to give her a reassuring smile, but his mouth refused to move. He knew they might need to hide and hide quickly. The silence attacked their ears. Zac scanned the interior frantically, where could they hide?

The two full-length barn door's opened, a man reached inside the Cargo van, he picked up a case of water bottles and he turned to leave.

A deep voice asked, "How many cases did you get?"

A higher tenor voice responded, "Just one, need more?"

Deep voice growled, "Yeah grab two more cases, those kids sure do go through the water."

Tenor said, "Okay, but let's get going. We're late for our shift."

Deep voice answered, "Okay, let's go then."

The slam of the two van's barndoors echoed inside the van as they closed.

A young high voice sounded out, "That sure was a close call."

A hand pulled back the heavy green tarp. "That's way too close for comfort. Thank God we found the tarp in time."

"Yes, thank God. Please Zac, call Mom or Dad so they can track your phone for our location."

"I'm on it Zoe." Zac tapped on a picture of Dad in a ranger uniform.

"Well...what's going on? If Dad's not answering, then call Mom."

As Zac touched the icon of his mother the screen faded away.

"Crap. We have a problem, nobody is going to answer, the phone is dead. The battery just ran out."

Zoe's voice raised even a higher pitch, "What!?!"

Looking down at the lifeless phone, Zac bit his lower lip. "Apparently during the storm, I took it off the charger to look at the weather and never reconnected it."

"Zac!..."

A different type of silence filled the van.

Lori had enjoyed the drive back to the motel, it was the first quiet moment she had had for the entire vacation. She loved her family dearly. But every now and then, even Moms need a timeout. She found herself actually cheerfully whistling a song as she got out of the Jeep and went to unlock the motel room door.

"Zac—Zoe, I'm back…. Hello?"

"Hello, it's Mom."

Closing the door, Lori looked around the room. "Not funny, you guys are too old to play hide and seek. Okay, I get it. The joke is on me. Get out here now. NOW!"

Placing her hands on her hips, Mom was ready to explode. " I left you two here alone because I trusted you. Come on out now. I mean now! I'm serious get out here or I will throw both your tablet's in the garbage."

Frowning Lori scanned the room.

Lori raced to the bathroom—no one. She got on a knee and looked under the three beds—no one. Her mind raced with many thoughts, options, and possibilities… her children were gone. When she got her hands on them, they were going to get it! Lori picked up the phone and started to call, but she knew better than to interrupt the meeting, so she texted Steven instead. Great. She had to play the waiting game for his return phone call.

Searching the room again, Lori hoped for a different result. She got a bottle of water and took a couple of sips to calm herself. She then went out to walk around and check out the parking lot. Next she orbited the entire motel building, looking in the lobby and game room, again nothing. Impatiently she texted Steven again, her nervous hands misspelling words.

She got the "CALL ME ASAP finally right.

Should she get in the Cherokee and drive around looking for them? If she left and Zac and Zoe came back what would happen? Then she realized that she being so upset, she didn't think to call Zac's cellphone. She mused, silly her she didn't think of that in the first place.

Lori called Zac's phone, it went straight to voicemail. That did not make her feel better. Her plush red lips turned into a frown, she was going to give it to those two kids of her. She called again—voicemail. Taking a deep breath, then Lori exhaled sharply. Should she stay by the room or go out again and look for them? Just then her phone rang, Steven's picture showed up. She tapped the icon.

"Hi honey, what's the urgency?"

Lori's voice exploded, "The kids are not here, I looked everywhere, the room, the parking lot, the grounds. I also called Zac's cellphone and…and it went to voicemail. They either left the room on their own--or something worse. We need to…" Her voice trailed off in the middle of the sentence, trying not to cry.

"It will be okay Loreli, did you check the lobby and the game room?"

"Of course, I did! I'm not incompetent and I'm not an idiot."

"I never said that."

"Sorry Steven, I'm just that upset. What do we do?"

"Maybe there's bad reception for his phone to work, or the battery ran out. Here's what we'll do, my meeting is over in an hour or so, stay there. I will get a ride from Joe. If they are still gone, I will call the Sheriff's department, but you know what they will say."

Sadly, Lori said, "Yes, but I know they half to be gone 24 hours to file a missing person's report."

"I have some say in the matter since I now know Deputy Sheriff Williams and I can get the Park Ranger department to help. We will get on it. Hang tight and I will see you in an hour or so.

"That's a long time to wait. What if something did happen to them?"

"They will be fine."

"But how can you know that?' Lori questioned.

Lori?"

"Yes."

Trying to use a reassuring voice, Steve said, "It will be okay, the kids will be safe."

Lori sighed, perhaps she sobbed, "I sure hope so. I will pray positively for their safe return. LYB."

"It will be okay. LYB." said Steven as he hung up.

No cell phone, no way of getting help, trapped in a van, were Zac and Zoe doomed? What would be their fate? Would Governor Meyer's kids be rescued?

CHAPTER 8

Meanwhile back inside the van: for the young Lund's the atmosphere seemed gloomy; their mood as dim as the lighting.

Trying to plan what to do, Zac sat in the van.

"When are we getting out Zac?" Zoe's hand tapping rapidly on the tarp they had been hiding under.

"I'm working on it." Zac summoned up his courage, this was going to be interesting. He somehow had to keep his sister positive.

Touching her brothers shoulder, "This is scary, we are all alone. Zac, you should have checked your phone battery."

"I know sis...I know." He snapped at Zoe, "You don't have to remind me." But deep down inside Zac was mad at himself for not checking.

Quickly Zoe withdrew her hand, "I'm sorry, but is a tough situation we're in."

"We will find a way out Zoe...and help the Meyers's kids."

"Ok bro, then let's go get help."

"Prepare yourself Zoe, I'm going to open the doors now."

"Okay bro, do it before I change my mind."

An instant blast of sunlight flooded their senses and attacked their eyes. A long time had been spent in the darkness of the van. The two youths blinked, rubbed their eyes, and blinked some more adjusting to the bright daylight. After a couple of moments, Zac peeked out between the barndoors of the van.

"Okay sis, I think the coast is clear."

Trying to be brave, "Lead on Zac."

The Lund's got out, or you could say they crawled out. Zac and Zoe crouched down and cautiously moved along the van using it as cover. They spied a wood cabin at the edge of a small dirt driveway where the Ford E-Transit van was parked. Zac pointed at some shrubbery and bushes. He started out with Zoe quickly following. They scurried over to the ground cover.

"Zoe, we need to get a good look inside the cabin to see if the Meyers's children are inside."

"That's easier said than done, bro."

"We will circle the cabin and find a window to look in."

Zoe's bright eyes pleaded with Zac, "Can I be honest? I'm scared. I might just stay here while you look."

Puzzled, but only for a moment, Zac said, "I've got an idea."

"What's that?" Zoe asked cautiously wondering about trusting her brother.

"The Meyers's boy's name is Waldo."

86

"That's right."

Zac rubbed his hands together, "Let's have a game, a game of finding Waldo. If you play a game, it will be easier on you."

"Really, finding Waldo? That's retarded." Zoe let the idea sink in for a moment. "Well…maybe it could work."

"Sure, it will work. Where is Waldo? Is he in the cabin?"

Signing, Zoe gave in, with a slight smile she pointed, "Let's go find out. I spy a window on that side."

Zac pointed out, "If I find Waldo first you owe me."

"I'm going to win Zac, you'll owe me big time."

"No, you will owe me." Zac wanted to get Zoe going.

The two Lund's sneaked over to the cabin window, Zoe being way too short to get a good look, she nodded upward. Zac took the hint and lifted her up to the windowsill.

"Zoe, what do you see?"

"A small bedroom, with a cot in it. No Waldo there. Zac, let's stop playing this game and let's get out of here."

"No, we can't stop looking till we find Waldo. Let's go to the next window." Zac lowered her and they slowly and noiselessly slid along the cabin wall to the back, there was another window.

"Where is Waldo? Is he inside the room behind this window? Can you see him?" Zac asked

Zoe looked at him thinking that he seemed ridiculous as older brothers often are.

Nodding, Zac played the game, "I thinking Waldo is behind this window. Once again."

Zoe shrugged shoulders; she said one word, "Really."

Hefting Zoe upward, she peered into the window, Zac asked, "Is Waldo inside, Zoe?"

She looked dejected and shook her head no. "You can put me down. Let's leave."

Trying to be positive, "Come on Zoe, Waldo will be behind the next window, I'm sure of it."

"He better be, Zac, it's the last window."

Taking Zoe's reluctant hand, Zac lead or more or less pulled her up to the window on her shoulders. "Up we go sis." Zac hoisted Zoe.

Okay, but be careful with me Zac."

Under his breath with his legs wobbling, Zac said, "You can trust me."

With his hand, Zoe wiped the glass of the cabin, she looked at Zac, her face shone with excitement.

"I see them!" Zoe exclaimed. "The Meyers's kids are in this room." Zoe frowned, "And...there is a huge woman with them."

A hand forcibly grabbed Zac's shoulder. A voice suddenly boomed out of now where, "What are you kids doing here? Are you spying? Get down girl—now!"

Zoe's head snapped backward at the man standing there. Quickly thinking Zoe's foot snapped into the man's nose, his nose turned bright red like Rudolph, the Red--Nose reindeer. He howled out in surprise and in pain.

Calling out, "Run, Zac—now!"

Zac tried to run, but the man's gripped Zac's shoulder in a rock hard grip. Zoe leaped out of Zac's arms, landing on her cat-like feet. She did a spinning heel foot sweep, striking the man's shin. Zac and the man tumbled downward, which should have freed Zac. The problem was that the man fell on top of Zoe's legs. The three became a mess of entangled legs and arms. Zac and the kidnapper thrashed about in the wet grass from the rain the night before. The sounds of yells, cries, groans, were mixed in with a few harsh words from the man.

Crying out, Zac said, "Get off me, get off me, get off meeee….."

In an act of desperation attempting to get himself and his sister free, Zac reached over and using two fingers he poked the man in his eyes. A bellow of pain erupted that echoed about the area. Zac and Zoe managing to get free jumped to their feet to scampered off like rabbits.

"Halt—right there, don't move a muscle! I don't care if you are kids. I'll blast you to pieces." The voice was mean, stern and well… kinda scary. The Lund's

89

froze in their tracks. They found themselves staring into the cold carbon steel barrel of a shotgun.

An eerie and creepy feeling went up their backs to have a shotgun aimed at them point blank. It seemed unreal, like a scene in a movie.

Holding his hands palms upward, Zac tried to look innocent, " We were just hiking in the woods and got lost. Honest. We found this cabin and we were going to knock on the door and ask for help."

Zoe piped in, "Yeah, it's a huge forest and these trees are kinda scary. Can you call our parents for us? They might even reward you." Her lower lip pouted, "Please call for us, we need help."

The chubby lady frowned, her red cheeks puffed up, like a blowfish. She looked at the man with the Rudolph, the reindeer red--nose.

The Rudolph man held both Zac and Zoe firmly by their shirt collars. He shrugged his shoulders. "I supposed they could be telling the truth; they could be lost. What do you think?"

Chubby's frown deepened, "It doesn't matter, we can't tack a chance. We have to deal with them—later. No loose ends. Into the cabin you go kids."

Rudolph followed along, "If you say so—no lose ends."

"But…but we were just hiking and got lost." Zac pleaded.

"Yeah." Siad Zoe agreeing. "It's a really big park. We just got lost, let us go."

No more games, you two kids get going. Into the cabin—now!"

She showed the way by the point of her shotgun. Zac knew now wasn't the time to try to escape and even if they did who would help save the Meyer's kids?

The only good Zac could think was getting inside the cabin would be one step closer to the problem. He wished to God that his cellphone worked. How stupid it is for him not to check the percent of the charge . Rudolph partially dragged them into the cabin, the two Lund's semi--resisting to make it look good. Inside the cabin, Rudolph half released, half tossed them to the hard wood floor. Zac and Zoe crashed harshly. But they did not lay there for long, they quickly rolled up to seated positions.

Putting on an act, Zac tried to argue. "You must let us go, we just got lost and we're scared. If we're gone for too long, our parent's will come looking for us."

"Yah, you better release us our dad is a forest...." Zac pinched Zoe's thigh unnoticed.

Zoe let out a, "Oh." Glaring at her brother.

"What was that for?" asked Rudolph.

Recovering quickly, Zoe claimed, "I just hurt my knee when I landed."

Chubby said, "Take their backpacks and toss them over there. She pointed. "Then frisk them for cellphones and stuff, I'll keep them covered."

Again, she scowled and waved the weapon of death and destruction at the two youths. They were searched, the cellphone was produced, but not much more. The two backpacks were thrown in the corner unopened. The Lunds were not so nicely scooted over to some seats by a wood table. Zac and Zoe looked at each other, Zoe wondering what to do. Zac nodded slightly no.

A bedroom door opened, the two men from the motel entered the room with Alexi and Waldo pushing them out in front. The men paused and looked at Zac and Zoe in surprise and wonder. They then advanced into the room and sat the Meyers's in two pine chairs by the table.

"What have we here? I thought I heard something. You guys have more kids."

"Hey!" the other man exclaimed, "Those kid's look familiar from somewhere? But from where?"

"They're from the Pine Tree Motor Lodge. You idiot!"

"How the heck did they get out here? And don't call me idiot, stupid."

Chubby broke in, "Stop it, they must have followed you two birdbrains."

Idiot asked, "How are kids going to follow us? They have no car. They couldn't have biked here."

"How about by dirt bike? Chubby asked.

"To noisy. We would have heard them. Idiot added.

"I agree." Stupid said, "I kept checking and know that we weren't followed."

Suggesting, Rudolph said, "Then they must have somehow hidden in your van, there is no other way they could have got here."

Idiot threw his hands up in despair. "How the heck are kids going to get in the van without us seeing them? We would have noticed."

"Yeah," Stupid agreed. "They're just kids, we would have heard them, and we opened the back once and nobody was there."

Rudely, Chubby said, "They sure didn't get here by helicopter."

But we know how Zac and Zoe arrived.

CHAPTER 9

The cabin grew noisy as the arguing started up between the four kidnappers. Their voices were louder and getting louder, blaming each other.

Whispering to Alexi and Waldo, "I'm Zac, this is my sister Zoe, we're here to help you escape."

Zoe added, "Yah, we're here to get you guy's out."

Wrinkling up her nose, Lexi declared. "That's ridiculous! No offence, but you're no older than us. How do you plan to get us out?"

Waldo looked at Zac and Zoe, to him they looked like ordinary kids. "We're doomed, we are never going to get out of here. I'll never see Mom and Dad again. I don't want to die in this lousy cabin."

Sarcastically, Zac said, "Thanks for the vote of confidence, Waldo."

"You know my name?"

Zoe's voice rose in frustration. "That's just what my brother Zac said, we're here to rescue you."

Guessing, Lexi asked "What are you 14 or 15? And Zoe you're around 11 or 12? You can't be any older than that. How are you two going to stop four ruthless kidnappers and a shotgun?"

"Yes, how are going win against a shotgun." Waldo asked.

Not wanting to admit it, but Zac had just turned 15 and Zoe was 12. He wanted Lexi and Waldo to trust him so he lied, "I'm 17 and we are highly trained in martial arts, if you don't believe we can save you, our dad is a Forest Ranger, and he will find us. Him and his fellow rangers are combing the woods for us right now." Another lie.

"You're not 17." Said Waldo defiantly.

"I have to agree with my brother."

For once Zoe said nothing, she knew she should let her brother work with Meyers's.

Zac stood up straight looking as serious as possible, "The important thing is we are here, and we will get you out. What choice do you have except to trust us? You two haven't escaped yet on your own accord."

Shaking her head in disbelief, Lexi interrupted, "That's uncalled for Zac, we can't escape, these kidnappers are pros. How did you find us? It just seems impossible for you guys to be here. You two weren't just out hiking and accidentally found us—tell me the truth."

With her green eye's glaring, Zoe stated, "My brother and I are here to rescue you. Don't you want to see your parents alive again?

Responding, Waldo stated, "No...I mean yes I want to see my parents, but I don't believe you two. And if Lexi and I get out of here alive, the kidnappers are going to kill you two, as they say in the movies, *no loose ends*."

"We don't want to die." Lexi was about to the point of tears.

The two Meyer's hugged each other.

Zac tried to talk but had to choked down the fear that he fought in the pit of his stomach, maybe they had bitten off more than they could chew. He couldn't let Zoe's death be his fault. Dad and Mom would kill him if that happened! He looked at Zoe, her face ash white, but her emerald eyes were bright and defiant.

Glancing over his shoulder, Zac saw Chubby standing there on the other side of the room gesturing with her hands telling off Stupid and Idiot for being followed. Which they of course they were denying. Rudolph stood there listening to Chubby, rubbing his sore red nose from Zoe's wicked kick.

Catching his breath and regained his nerves, Zac briefly explained about the motel and the van ride and Zoe told them about finding Lexi's necklace. Zac and Zoe wisely skipped the part about finding the dead F.B.I. man.

Looking downward, then Lexi slowly up at the Lunds. "So that's what happened to my necklace, I knew I lost it somewhere and that clue led you to us."

Waldo said, "That's so weird it must be true. You guys think you can actually get us out of here?"

"Sure, piece of cake." Replied Zac. Trying to even convinced himself that is would be that easy. Zac then looked at Zoe.

"I got it!" Zoe whispered something into Zac's ear.

Agreeing Zac whispered back to Zoe.

Zoe whispered once more. Zac shook his head in agreement.

The Meyers's curiosity arose, Lexi and Waldo lightly chanted in more of a whisper, "Tell us, tell us, tell us."

"Rather than tell you, we will show you." Zac abruptly shoved Zoe, her and the pine chair went crashing to the hardwood floor."

She bellowed out, "I hate you Zac! Why did you push me? You're so mean."

Jumping to his feet, "You're a brat and always bugging me, you're so annoying."

"You're the annoying one, Zac."

"Little sisters are little sister. You just shut your mouth."

"I will not, you shut your trap."

"I will punch you Zoe if I have to."

"I tell Mom and Dad. Just stop it."

The Lund's bickered and started yelling loudly and arguing. It looked like they were going to get into a fight.

Chubby grimaced, bit her lower lip and nodded to the men, "Quiet them down-now!"

"Yeah, shut both of them up." Rudolph ordered.

Idiot and Stupid headed over to the table. Zac and Zoe were wrestling around with each other, yelling, and making a terrible fuss. Lexi and Waldo sat there, their jaws hanging open at the sight of the Lund's fighting each other. Zac picked up a chair and started to swing it at Zoe, at the last possible second, he changed direction, swinging it, hitting Idiot against his right shoulder. Zoe pretended to duck under the chair and foot swept Stupid who spilled onto his butt. Chubby waddled over to grab her shotgun, Rudolph stood there rubbing his sore nose, not knowing whether to laugh or get concerned.

Zoe crawled over behind Idiot, stopped perched on her hands and knees. Zac shouted "ki-yah" and side kicked Idiot in his stomach. He fell backwards, tripped over Zoe, and hit the ground so hard, that his head bounced twice off the wood floor. Ouch!

"I'll get both of those brats." Idiot bellowed.

Stupid got to his feet and charged Zac, who did a judo hip flip. Stupid's own momentum did the rest; he flew into a cabin wall, collapsed, and laid there stunned. Lexi looked at both the Lund's in amazement, Zac and Zoe had just taken out two kidnappers. Maybe, just maybe, they could be rescued, but things can change fast. Chubby reached the shotgun; Rudolph started to rush over to stop the Lund's with his hands outstretched.

As Chubby started to picked up the shotgun and yelled, "You brats, stop now or I will shoot both of you!"

Zac raced toward Chubby and her shotgun. The youth launched a flying side kick that would have made Batman's sidekick, Robin proud. He landed on the shotgun at about the same time Chubby hand had touched the shotgun. The gun skittered along the floor and a shot went off.

KA-BOOM!

The sound was amplified inside the wood cabin, everyone's ears rang at the sound of the shot. Unnoticed, Zoe made it to her backpack and pulled out a large aerosol container. She bound over to the front door of the cabin.

"Lexi and Waldo get over here now! Get behind me." Zoe pointed the cannister at Rudolph.

Pushing against Chubby Zac attempted to free himself. Chubby seemed more concerned about getting the shotgun than grabbing Zac, which was a major mistake! Zac broke free, sprinted over to Zoe, and stood beside her.

"Zoe. Now!"

"Okay Brother!"

Zoe let Rudolph have it full blast, bear pepper spray in the face. Poor Rudolph never had a chance. A cloud of red pepper oil, called capsaicin filled the cabin, Rudolph's nose turned even redder if that was possible. He stopped dead in his tracks, coughing and convulsing. His hands frantically rubbing at his eyes. The cloud of pepper expanded over to Chubby who also started hacking and gagging. The shotgun lay on the floor useless and untouched. Zac opened the door just in time as the spray engulfed the room. The four youth's spilled out the cabin door to fresh air and sunshine! They coughed and gagged some from the spray, but they were promptly outside.

"I apologize," said Lexi. "For doubting you. You two were absolutely amazing!"

Zoe said, "You should see our Uncle Scott in action, if you want to see amazing."

Rubbing his hands together, Waldo said, "That was really cool."

"No time for talk gang." barked Zac. "We need to go now while we still can. Let's make a break for it."

"Follow Zac!" Zoe yelled.

Instantly, Zac took off for the woods. Because of the massive rain the night before the grass and weeds were slippery and wet, which made their going difficult. The four youths made their way to the woods painfully slow. With the feeling of every minute expecting the cabin to eject the kidnappers, or worse yet, the sound of a gunshot.

They were almost to the woods now, so far, so good or so they hoped. Then it happened, Lexi slipped and fell. Zac abruptly stopped, bent over and held out his hand, "Come on we need to go."

Lexi hesitated to take Zac's hand. *Who is this teen and his sister? Where were they taking her and her brother?*

BOOM!

Chubby stood in the cabin doorway. A puff of smoke now melting upward into the big blue sky. She took aim again, preparing to fire. Who was she aiming at? Zac knew it wasn't at the Meyer kids, they were worth too much money.

"Quick!" Urged Zac, "Give me your hand."

With her eyes wide open in fear, Lexi grabbed Zac's hand.

Waldo and Zoe were at the edge of the clearing, impatiently waiting. Lexi clutched Zac's hand, he yanked Lexi to her feet in one swift move. Off they raced to the woods.

KA—BOOM!

A tree branch broke off a meter from Zac's sandy--haired head. Splinters of wood and shards of tree bark exploded outward a few landing on the youths. Lexi ducked in a reflex move that almost resulted in the two youths falling to the ground. The two of the men raced out the door to the back of a cabin where an outbuilding was located. Zac had noted it but was unsure what it contained.

Chubby stood there holding the smoking shotgun, yelling foul words at them, Rudolph next to her looking miserable, wiping his face with a cloth, his nose redder than ever.

Chubby screamed at the top of her healthy lungs, "Get back here—there will be no more warning shots. Stop now!"

She leveled her lethal weapon and aimed at Zac. She shouted, "Last chance Kids or else."

Rudolph also yelled, "Stop of else."

101

Idiot and Stupid just stood there confused on what to do.

"Into the woods--now," A frantic Zac commanded.

How could his parents forgive him if harm came to his sister Zoe? After all, he was the big brother. The four youths ducked into the dense redwood trees, their thick cinnamon colored bark glistening with wetness from last night's storm. The echo of the shotgun sounded, announcing that another shot had been fired. The Lund's and Meyers's ran the best they could for about fifteen minutes, no more telltale shotgun shots were heard. They stopped behind a mound of shrubbery, their breaths ruff and ragged from the adventure thus far.

CHAPTER 10

Huffing and puffing the youths were hiking as a brisk pace. Zac spoke, "I think we got away at least for the moment."

"Can we take a break to catch our breaths?" Asked Lexi.

"Yeah, just a short breather." Waldo said panting.

"Okay, but we can only rest for a couple of minutes and then we move out." Zac replied.

"We need to follow Zac." Zoe panted excitedly. "We can't stop now."

While Lexi leaned against a tree regaining her breath, she took stock of Zac and Zoe, "I must admit I am shocked that you got us out of there. You two are like a pair of 'power twins.'"

Shaking his head in disbelief, Waldo said, "Great job, getting us out of the cabin. I almost believe I won't die—at least not now."

Waldo fist bumped Zac and Zoe.

Zoe said, "Sorry guys, I don't want to be a downer, but we are still in trouble. There is a creek ahead of us and with the flashflood this morning, it's too high and dangerous to cross. What are we going to do Zac?"

"Give me a second everybody. I will check the creek.

Wandering over to the creek, Zac saw that the current was torrential, the water was foamy, frothy, and angry. It looked insurmountable, with no way to cross it. They all would drown for sure.

Waldo whined, "I'm not a good swimmer."

In a trembling voice, Lexi said, "Nobody can swim across in that current."

"We have to try something, what else do we to go?" Zoe said trying to brave.

Zac knew both he and Zoe were excellent swimmers, but trying to cross a flooded creek was like asking to be drowned. He sprinted up and down the bank, to no avail. The creek by last night's rain had now turned into a raging river.

Stopping, Zac addressed the group. "We have to head right, or left, we can't go back."

"We can't make it." Lexi exclaimed.

Literally jumping up and down in fear, Waldo screeched, "Let's make a run down along the stream."

"The kidnappers will be sure to catch up that way." Zoe stood ready at run to Waldo's side to grab his arm in case he would start running away.

The four youth's stood by confounded on what to do.

A roar was heard, and it didn't come from the raging stream that seemed more like a river. It was the roar of an engine. The group stared backwards; it was not a pretty sight. A green ATV hurtled toward them, in it held the four kidnappers in a John Deere Gator. The youths saw Chubby leaning out with her shotgun, a maniacal gleam upon her face. A look of Death!

Zac faced the raging white rapids on the water, his face resolved. "We have to go! There is no more time."

Lexi was panicking now, "Do what now? We can't cross the stream."

Waldo ran to his sister's arms. "What do we do, Sis?"

Zac focused on analyzing the stream; many logs were floating down it. A log about ten meters long raced and bobbed down the stream. "We jump for it!"

"Jump for what?" Then Zoe read Zac's mind, "That's it we take a ride on the log, it's our ticket out of here!"

Lexi shook her head profusely, "NO WAY!"

Going over to Waldo, Zoe said, "Take my hand, we will jump together. You can do it."

"No way I'm not jumping on a log. That's crazy." Waldo started to edge backward from the stream.

Zac grabbed Lexi and started dragging her to the foamy water's edge. Above the sound of roaring water, Zac implored, "You have to trust us, it's the only way out. Do you want to get shot? Jump when I say jump."

Lexi stood frozen like a deer in the headlights. Zac slapped her face, it wasn't a gentle slap, but a slap powerful just enough to bring Lexi back to her senses.

Touching her flushed and reddened cheek she said only one word. "Okay."

"The same to you Waldo, we have to go." Zoe said the words to encourage herself as well as Waldo.

A voice cried out, it came from Stupid. "There they are! Stop them! They can't get away and notify the authorities."

"You heard the man get going." Chubby commanded.

The Gator raced toward them with the four kidnapper in it. Leaning out of it was Chubby ready to fire another shot. Rudolph sat in back, slumped over gasping and holding his painful Rudolph-red nose. Idiot bore down at them now driving like a mad man, the Gator hopping up and down over the rough terrain. The four youths all held hands ready for one word…

Zac screamed at the top of his lungs, "JUMP!"

The four youths jumped, eight arms went up in the air and eight legs sprung upward…. They landed on a long 'deadhead', a waterlogged piece of timber, mostly submerged. Desperately, the youths were frantically clutching and grabbing at the knobs of the log for their lives, which they were. For if they stayed behind or fell off, death awaited them, either drowning in raging water or at the end of a shotgun! That is if Chubby got her way with them.

Miraculously no one fell off, adrenaline adding strength to their grips on the log. For they were on the ride of their short young lives. They jostled up and down in the white-water rapids, at a speed of almost 20 kilometers per hour. Deep down inside, half of the ride seemed scary and terrifying, to the Lunds, but somehow the other half of it was thrilling and fun! But Lexi and Waldo had masks of terror on their faces.

Zac wanted to hoot and holler like a cowboy on top of a wild horse. He called out, "Everybody hand on tight for your dear lives!"

"You heard my brother Zac. Hang on!"

"Okay." Gulped Waldo.

With her teeth clenched, Lexi said nothing.

Zac dared to take a quick glance backward as they raced done the flooded creek. Looking backward he could make out the silhouette green of the John Deere Gator. Suddenly Zac didn't like the color green anymore. Lexi and Waldo were grim and silent, their knuckles white from grasping onto the bobbing 'deadhead.' Somehow in the midst of all the turmoil, Zoe had a smile on her face, her green eyes bright and alive. Inside Zac marveled at his sister's bravery, but he would never say anything to her about it.

BOOM!

The harsh sound of a shotgun blast brought Zac back to the chilling reality of their life and death situation. A chunk of wood exploded from the front of the log, followed by the spray of water. Lexi and Waldo screamed, Zoe clung tighter to the log, lowering her profile. All Zac could do, is to hope the stream would curve and take them out of sight from the kidnappers and the aim of the shotgun. But where did the roaring stream go? Did it come to an end or take them out to another body of water? Time would tell if they lived long enough. For the next minute a blur of pine, red fir trees, bushes, and shrubbery went by. The beautiful wildflowers along the bank went unnoticed. Again, the frightening sound of a shotgun erupted over the roar of the raging stream.

An innocent lodgepole pine tree took the shotgun blast, bark and chunks of wood went flying off, a jagged hole appeared in the trunk. The Gator speedily closing in at a much faster speed than the log. Things were beyond desperate now, the next shot would probably not miss. The youths could see Chubby and her shotgun clearly; by now she had pumped the gun ready to fire again. Unexpectedly the Gator hit a stump and lurched sideways, Chubby flailed about knocked off balance and almost got tossed out of the AVT. Zac wanted to cheer, but somehow Chubby had regained her balance. Zac's heart leaped to his throat, what now?

The answer came unexpectedly, quite a surprise in fact, Zac thought for sure it wasn't good. Ahead of them a fallen tree crossed over the stream, and they were on a collision course with it. What could they do? There could be no turning back, could they leap off the 'deadhead' and make the bank?

The green Gator raced back on a course to intercept them. This was it! The end for all four of them. Zac felt stupid and foolish to think they could

108

follow the kidnapper's and save the Meyers's. He and Zoe would be finished—forever. It would be on his head that Zoe died, inside he knew he loved her, but he couldn't now tell her. He would never live to see Dad and Mom again, what had he done?

Frantically scanning around for anything to help, Zac elevated his gaze and saw a shape in a tree, an open platform? There in the tree sat a large hunting stand. If they could just somehow reach it?

The tree stood aways before the fallen tree blocking their escape. He started yelling, to get everybody's attention over the sound of the raging water.

"Everybody listen up!" He cried out. "We jump to the left! Try to make it to the deer stand!"

Nobody had to be told twice to get off this wild ride, especially with a crazy woman shooting at them. The log swirled sideways somewhat closer to the bank, they leaped off and landed on the shoreline clinging to underbrush and vines.

Waldo's grip failed as the dirt bank crumbled. He started sliding backwards into the racing current, a look of panic painted on his face. "H…He…Help!"

"Save my brother." Screamed Lexi. "Somebody save him!"

STAY TUNED FOR THE EXCITING CLIMAX OF
MYSTERY AMONG THE TREES!

CHAPTER 11

A hand clutched his shoulder, then a second hand clasped his other shoulder, the Lund's somehow in spite of the velocity of the water managed to pull Waldo up on the shore. Waldo laid there gasping and puffing. So terrified he couldn't even speak and say thanks to the Lund's.

Half wet and plenty scared the Lund's and Meyers's climbed up off the bank, then to the temporary safety of land. They were still not out of harm's way, there being a problem because the bank the tree stand was on the same side of the kidnappers and the oncoming Gator.

Zac and Zoe started yelling at the Meyers's, urging them to climb up the ladder to the tree stand. Lexi and Waldo were dazed, confused and they were not climbing. Zac resisted kicking them in their behinds to get them going.

Looking at Zac, Zoe's face flushed with excitement, "Do we climb, or do we stay and try to hold them off?"

Looking at his sister's somehow calm face, Zac said, "Zoe you remind me of Mom at this moment. No, we have to climb up there, then get the Meyers's going up to the tree stand and hope for a rescue. Dad and his Forest Rangers should by now be looking for us."

Although Zac knew the chances were next to slim and next to none that Dad and the rangers were actually nearby.

"I remind you of our Mother?"

"We can get into that later. Let's get going."

Confused for the moment, Zoe had to let that go. "Okay, we can talk about it later. That is if we live to talk about it."

"Yeah let's go with that."

Chiming in Lexi agreed. "Let's get the four of us out of here alive."

"I want to live, I want to see Mom and Dad again." Then trying to be brave, Waldo straightened up. "We can do this, we can get out of here alive. Right!"

Slapping him on the shoulder, Zac said, "That's the right attitude."

"Good job Waldo. That's my brave brother."

"Let's get going everybody." Zoe pointed to the tree.

Lexi and Waldo started to climb, at a rate far to slow for Zac and Zoe. Zac urged them on. Once the Meyers's were halfway up, the Lund's scampered up the ladder like monkeys being chased by tigers. Which isn't far from the truth. The Gator drove right up to the base of tree, all four kidnappers clambered out and they raced to the base of tree. Rudolph tried to say something but couldn't because his throat was still roached from the pepper spray.

111

Taking charge, Chubby commanded, "Come on down kids, right now and we might let some of you live."

The youths stood there looking down in bleak silence.

"Well, if you don't come down." Chubby said slowly savoring the moment, "Or I can shoot you one at a time and see who I save for last."

Zac spat at her, a loogy hit her left shoulder. The four kids laughed in spite of the situation. Chubby's face turned bright red, her cheeks puffed. "I will save you for last young man, in fact, I might only shoot you one leg at a time."

Zac gulped.

In a last act of defiance, Zoe picked up a fallen branch off the tree stand floor and whipped it downward. Guess who it hit? Of course, it hit poor Rudolph on his nose. He yelped, it looked like he was going to cry.

It's amazing what Mother Nature can do at times and in this case, at the right time. There came the sound of water lashing at the banks and trees. A breaker wave, much like a tidal wave came rolling down the already engorged stream. A towering wall of water raged toward them; it swelled over the banks wiping out plants, vegetation, and undergrowth.

Chubby screamed, "Oh no!"

Idiot and Stupid echoed her words.

Rudolph bit his lower lip so hard it turned red like his nose.

Seeing their fate, the three men cursed, and yelled, then they were no more. The kidnappers all wiped out, like they had been flushed down the toilet by nature!

All that was left behind stood the water-soaked Gator with plants and leaves scattered on it. The four youths stood frozen, they were mortified by the mammoth wave that had just saved them. They watched the wave continue down the foaming stream, destroying bushes, shrubs, and trees, consuming everything in its wake. Then as quickly as it arrived, the wave receded and disappeared. So did the roar of fury. The Lund's and the Meyers's were spent, they collapsed on their rearends on the floor of the tree stand. They sat there frozen in shock and amazement at the event that just occurred.

What just happened? Could it have been a dream...or a nightmare?

Thirty minutes or so later, two vehicles rolled in. The two green SUV's had Yosemite State Park markings. The doors opened and four men in Park Ranger uniforms got out, two had shotguns. They went down to the river scouting around for signs of the kidnappers. After a few minutes of walking the rangers had reached the kids in the tree stand.

A worried voice called out, Zac, Zoe are you okay?"

"Dad? Dad it is you?" a teary-eyed Zoe answered from the tree stand.

"I'm so glad that you're here." To say the least Zac finally felt relieved.

Steven had already spotted them earlier in the tree stand when they were driving around. "Come on down guys. Wow! Is that the Meyers's children with you?"

"Yes, here we are." stated Lexi.

Loudly announcing to the rangers, "I'm Waldo Meyers. Our Daddy is the Governor of California."

Steven approached the tree stand, and by his side stood Ranger Joe Hartley. Joe in his right hand held a pair of bino's, both men had firearms holstered on their belt. Steven stopped at the base of the tree stand perched over the drenched John Deere ATV. He peered into the Gator, seeing it sat empty.

He called out, "Nobody's here, where are the kidnappers?"

Answering back, Zac said, "You won't believe the story I have for you when we get down. It's a whopper."

Zoe had to agreed, "Yeah, Dad, it's sick."

Coning his hand by his mouth, Steven shouted, "Come on down—all of you."

Alexia and Waldo had stood up, but they were like froze like statues. Zoe urged them forward, but shock had set in, and they were afraid to climb down the ten-meter ladder. Going up the ladder had been much easier, especially being chased and fearful for your life.

Ranger Joe approached the ladder and put his left hand on a rung. "Do you need help? I can climb up there."

Zac leaned over, "Naw, I got this covered. We'll be right down."

Zoe agreed, "We can make it."

"We will make it."

Zac gently took Lexi's arm and gave her a slight tug. She stood there numb and expressionless. "Lexi, it's safe now—time to climb down."

Her head tiled slightly; she blinked a few times.

Pulling on her harder, Zac coached her, "Lexi it's time to go. Come on, let's climb down the ladder. It will be okay. I'll go with you."

Not moving a muscle, Lexi stood still dazed, Dr. Lori had given her two children basic medical training, so he could see shock was setting in. Zac massaged her wrist's briskly, she mumbled something. Yet, Lexi just stood there.

Having an opportunity, Zac took it. He grabbed Lexi and planted a kiss on her, fully on the lips. Stunned at first, then Lexi reciprocated, for a long moment, their arms wrapped around each other. The two fifteen-year old's seem to be enjoying the moment. Zoe's mouth dropped open at the sight.

Covering his eyes, Waldo said, "Eck."

Rushing to the base of the ladder. Steven shouted upward. "Zacary Lund, stop it, this moment!"

The embrace and kiss ended, Lexi looked shocked but in a different way. She looked star struck. Zac had a smile on his face; so big that it would take a week to wipe it off. Zoe punched Zac hard in the shoulder snapping him out of his trance, but Zac still kept smiling.

Thinking out loud, "I just kissed a governor's daughter."

Frowning, Zoe took Waldo's hand, "Waldo, let's get out of here."

Eventually they did get Zac and Lexi down, Steven and Joe had to more or less pry the Meyers's out of the tree stand. Zac and Zoe explained about the fight, and the bear spray in the cabin. Then the shotgun chase and of course the mighty wave that washed away the existence of the four kidnappers. The kidnappers' bodies would be found downstream later that day by a search party. Somehow miraculously the shotgun had been wedged in a tree branch about 3 or 4 meters above the ground.

Wrinkling his forehead, Steven listened in disbelief at the incredible story Zac and Zoe had told him. His wife Lori was going to be furious and go ballistic when she found out what Zac and Zoe did. Nothing like the wrath of a mother. Then the story about Zac and Zoe climbing in the van, spying into the cabin and getting captured. But they did escape and rescue the Meyers's children. Proudly Steven did an inward smile,

After all, Zac and Zoe had been successful and there had been a "Happy Ending."

116

How mad could Mom get?

CHAPTER 12

"Dad, I'm nervous."

"It will be okay son; you'll be just fine." Reassured Steven in his deep voice. He placed his hand on Zac's shoulder. "After everything you did on your wild adventure, you're now telling me your nervous?"

"Me too, Dad and Mom." Zoe said. "It is a bit nerve-racking to meet a governor. "I've never met a *real* Governor before."

"You both will be fine." comforted Lori. "He just wants to meet you two and say thanks for rescuing his children."

"After the wild adventure you guys went through, meeting a governor is no big deal." Dad said hoping to calm them down.

The sound of the turning doorknob and a creak announced the massive oak door opening. A tall lanky middle-aged man stood in the doorway, dressed a business two-piece dark blue suit. His dark black hair brushed back with a ring of grey around his ears.

"Hello, I'm Governor William Meyer's, you must be the Lund family. So good to meet you." He beckoned with his hand, "Please, please come into my office."

And what an office it was!

In one corner on a stand stood the American flag. In the other corner rested the California state flag, white with a wide red stripe on the bottom, a large grizzly bear facing left dominated the middle. From the domed ceiling dangled a gorgeous crystal chandelier. A mammoth cherry desk dominated the middle of the room, with dark red stuffed leather chairs forming a semi-circle. Beautifull oil paintings of nature lined the walls, with a large bay window on the far wall. The four Lund's entered the room, a blonde secretary stood ready by the desk with a drink cart. Introductions and greetings were made.

Sitting down, Governor Meyers's motioned to them to have a seat, "Would anyone like a beverage? Coffee, tea, soda, or milk? Even cookies? Anything at all."

The Lund's accepted coffee and the children said yes to milk and Zac and Zoe took a least a cookie or two. Who could blame them?

Spreading out his hands and gestured as politicians do, Willaim Meyers said, "From the bottom of our hearts my wife Carol, and I want to thank you for the rescue of Alexandra and Waldo. Zac and Zoe were spectacular from what they told me. The rescue seemed adventuresome—incredulous to say the least. A wild waterlog ride and a roller wave that wiped out the kidnappers. Their bodies were identified, they were the ones that...er eliminated the F.B.I. agent, Craig Mulden. His body has been discovered and recovered as well. Bad business! Mulden was on the trail of my children, and apparently he got too close. William shrugged his shoulders, "And you can guess the rest."

Lowering their heads, the Lund family was saddened by the memory of the deceased agent .

Finally, Zac broke the silence and said, "So we weren't crazy after all telling Dad and Mom we found a body."

Zoe corrected him, "Zac, I was the one that found the body."

"It seemed hard to swallow at first, but we did believe both of you." Lori said and touched her daughters shoulder.

"We did finally believe it." Steven added, "Because your mother and I have faith and trust in you two."

Governor Meyers's spoke up, "Lexi told me how you used bear pepper spray to confuse the kidnappers and escape. That was a brilliant move and then you two took out a couple of kidnappers. You are trained in the martial arts?"

Looking at each other, Zac and Zoe nodded to the Governor.

"That was smart Zoe. I had to use the pepper spray the day before to fend off a Momma bear."

Steven stated, "Yes, Zac and Zoe are both trained in Shotokan and Jui-jitsu, and so am I, sir."

"Did I hear Shotokan?" The door had opened, a sandy hair man entered, a slightly shorter and thicker version of Steven. His clothes could not hide the muscular physique and dynamic presence he brought with him into the room.

Zac and Zoe jumped to their feet, Lori tried to tell them to remain seated. Ignoring their mother, both Zoe and Zac ran over; Zoe hugged Uncle Scott who returned Zoe's hug. Zac fist bumped him—hard. Scott unglued Zoe from his brother. Scott went over and gave Lori a brief kiss on the cheek.

She warmly said, "Hello."

Walking over, Scott stood behind Steven, then he firmly placed his hand on Steven's left shoulder.

Smiling in acknowledgement, "Good to see you bro."

"Like wise." Scott addressed Zac and Zoe, "Great job you two, you're heroes."

Zac and Zoe's faces lit up like a Christmas tree.

Looking solemn faced, Zac said, "Thanks Uncle Scott, that does means a lot coming you."

Giving her smile, Zoe made a heart shape with her hands, "Thanks."

Returning her smile. "That's what Uncles are for."

The Governor's face beamed, he had read all about the story of Lund rescuing the President in a battle at a Superchurch in lower California last year. "You must be, Scott Lund, *the Border Patrol agent*."

Marginally, Scott nodded but said nothing.

Steven said, "Glad you made it Scott, it means a lot to the family." Zac and Zoe nodded in agreement.

Humbly, Scott replied, "Thanks for the invite, it's not every day I get to meet the Governor."

Circling his vast desk, Governor Meyers rose and extended his hand to Scott. "Great to meet you."

"The pleasure is mine." replied Scott in his baritone voice.

The two men eyed each other and shook hands firmly and briskly.

"Thank you for taking time out of your busy schedule to be here. You weren't saving the President today, were you?"

Scott chuckled, "Not today, at least not the United States President."

The Governor almost thought for a moment that Scott must be serious, then he chuckled too. "That's a good one."

William Meyers, then went over to Zac and Zoe.

The Governor bent forward warmly saying, "What you did was special. Who knows if we would have gotten our children back, even if we paid the ransom. You two saved Alexandra and Waldo's lives."

Zac looked up at the Governor, "We did what we had to do, it wasn't anything special. We were brought up to respect life and to save it."

"Yeah," said Zoe. "Our parents taught us that we're supposed to love people and honor them."

Straightening up, the Governor was taken aback by the simple truth and honesty of Zac and Zoe. They had simply done what they needed to do. He apparently had more work to do with his own children.

"I see. I will complement both of you and your parents."

Holding hands, Steven and Lori looked at their children.

Being serious, Zac said, "Sir, it took guts to get in that van, and I can't say I wasn't scared, but somebody had to save them. Sometimes you jump into the deep end of a pool, it forces you to swim out."

Moving over and standing behind his sister, "Zoe had a lot to do with the rescue too, I couldn't have done it without her. I'm not a one-man army like Uncle Scott." He ruffled her hair trying to hide how much he thought of Zoe.

Smiling slightly, Scott uncomfortably shuffled his feet, but he felt proud of his nephew and niece.

Zoe pretended to frown and be annoyed by Zac. "Dad and Mom always say we should make each other better and stronger."

Tilting her head, Lori wanted to make sure she was hearing correctly. "So, you guys do listen— sometimes."

All of the Lund's laughed.

Zoe confessed, "Yes, Mom we always listen and sometimes we get it."

Having to agree, Zac said, "It's not always easy to obey everything you and Dad say.

Steven rolled his eyes upward, "That's an understatement."

Both Zac and Zoe started talking fast, semi-arguing and semi-agreeing. Dad and Mom jumped right in. Willaim stood there watching the Lund's interact, taking it all in. He cleared his throat, the Lund's quit talking.

"You Lund's are an a most interesting family indeed." He walked back to his desk. My family and I can never fully show our full appreciation for what Zac and Zoe did."

The Governor nodded to his secretary, and she handed him an envelope. He presented it, "Thank you once again. Here is a gift for your family."

"Your welcome, but we don't need a gift."

Steven said, Zac blurted out, "But Dad…"

Being a mom, Lori interrupted, "You did not help save Alexandra and Waldo for a present."

William held up his hand, "It's okay, I understand youth, but I do insist Mrs. Lund that it would mean a lot to accept this gift." He held up a marigold-colored envelope. Zac and Zoe please come here."

They jumped to their feet, caught themselves and then calmly walked up to the Governor.

Solemnly, he handed the envelope to Zac and Zoe. Zac snatched it before Zoe could. The desk phone rang, William looked at it annoyed. He nodded, the secretary picked it up and spoke in undertones. She glanced at the Governor.

"You can open it up when you want to."

Standing up, Steven said, "Thank you, we will our own time, your busy. Let's go everybody, Uncle Scott is buying everybody pizza."

"I am? Oh, of course I am. Let's go to the Batmobile."

Hearing that, Governor Meyers made a polite smile. He said, "Goodbye everybody and thanks again."

Turning away, the Governor picked up the phone and started talking, his attention already diverted.

Out marched the Lund's into the hall and then through the state capitol building, out to the parking lot, into a bright cool clear Californian day. They went across the pavement and made it to the Jeep Cherokee.

Holding the envelope tightly, finally, Zac burst out, "Can we, can we please open it? Please?"

Zoe also asked, "Yes, please let's open the envelope, I just gotta know what's inside."

Stepping in, Scott joked in a kid's voice; "Come on, come on everybody, I want to see what's inside. Dad!"

Steven could only say one word, "Okay."

"Really? It's okay Dad."

Steven nodded yes.

Literally tore open the envelope, Zac looked inside. It contained a motel voucher and four passes.

Reading it, Zac showed it to Zoe who squealed in excitement.

Saying out loudly, Zac exclaimed, "Looks like we're going to Disney Land!"

The end for now.

Stay tuned for the further Lund Family Mysteries!

Don't Fall In!

Story by Raegan Marie Olson

Written by Dr Richard A. Olson

LUND FAMILY MYSTERIES

CHAPTER 1

"Put Rosie away."

"Mom, do I have to?"

"Right now, young lady." Taking her eyes off the HUD display on the cockpit windshield Lori gave Zoe the Mom look.

"All right Mom. Rosie, kennel up—now."

The dog, a large collie whined, it deep brown eyes pleaded with Zoe, a young girl of about 12. Zoe's bright green eyes met the collie's brown eye stare.

"Rosie kennel up, let's go girl. Hup, hup!"

The dog sat down on its hind legs.

"Kennel up Rosie--now.

Not wanting to miss anything, Rosie stayed put.

The girl frowned, her nose wrinkled, she took the dog firmly by the collar and placed her inside a grey plastic kennel, she rubbed the dog's long snout affectionately. "You need to obey, stay."

"After you take care of Rosie get in your seat Zoe and buckle up."

"You got it Mom."

"Thanks dear."

As Zoe prepared to close and latch the kennel door, a loud bang from the belly of the plane sounded. The wind turbulence increased as the planes landing flaps were brought into use. Rapidly Zoe closed and latched the kennel door. She raced to her seat and buckled up. The single jet engine of the Cirrus Vision's turbine sound increased as the pilot Lori reversed the engine thrust to slow down the aircraft. Pushed forward in the crate by the planes rapid deceleration, Rosie whined and let out a small bark for a dog as large as a collie.

Enjoying the ride, Zoe smiled with glee. Flying with Mom is always a treat. Mom being Dr Lorelie Lund, a famous exotic animal veterinarian. Her plane was a state of the art Willaims FJ33-5A a five seater single engine jet with 1,800 pounds of thrust. It's range was over 1600 kph and could cruse up to almost 600 kph. Their trip was soon ending with arrival in Tamaulipas airport near Mante, Mexico only a few minutes away.

Rapidly tapping the Garmen touch screen avionics a few times, Lori firmly took control of the wheel. She spoke Spanish into her headset microphone. A voice in Spanish answered back.

Growling uncomfortably in her kennel, Rosie did not like the sound or the planes vibrations.

Snapping her fingers Zoe said, "Enough of that girl we'll be landing soon. Don't worry, Mom's a great pilot."

The dog laid it's head down on its forepaws in the kennel, calmed by Zoe's high voice. The turbulence sounded louder and the bang, bang of the landing wheels were heard. Mom's voice rose in worry. Rapidly Lori spoke back and forth in Spanish to the control tower voice.

"Hang on tight Zoe, there's a flock of flamingos between us and the runway. This could be tricky."

"A flock of flamingos. How cool is that."

"It won't be cool if we hit a bunch."

Zoe hadn't thought of that.

Mom's hand went to the throttle and pulled back as she powered up the turbine engine. Zoe was thrown back into her seat as the plane lifted upward.

"Que Malo!" Lori yelled.

Understanding enough Spanish. Zoe asked, "Is it that   bad,   Mom?"
"Large birds can cause lots of damage especially to the engine blade and can affect the air flow."

"Are we going to crash? Mom will we be okay?"

Keeping her face calm. "No sweetie, I'll motor up, bank around, and come in on a different angle. We'll be okay."

"What if we get bird poop on the plane? Zoe giggled.

Mom had to join in and laugh. "When we get back to the States we will have Dad and Zac clean up the mess."

"Yeah, Mom." Zoe's imagination was running. "It will be great to see them get the poop off the windshield."

Both females had a good laugh, and by the way for the plane did land safely. No birds were injured, and we won't mention the poop.

Several hours later. "Reservations for the Lund's. Lori asked.

"Welcome to the Hotel Capybara. Si, si, here we are." The Hispanic man was looking at the monitor behind the counter, he raised his eyes. "You are Dr. Lund, the veterinarian. They call you Dr. Lori...Si?"

Lori's gaze met him straight on. "Yes I am. Do I know you?"

"No-no Senora, but once you did help my cousin, he had Spider monkeys, some of them were sick, you attended and aided them. He showed me some pictures of you working."

The doctor snapped her fingers, "Of course, the Rancho de Martinez, I remember Juan now. How is he doing?"

The hotel clerk smiled almost ear to ear. "Wonderful! It will be much pleasure to serve you…Si. In fact, we will upgrade you to a special suite on the main floor."

"You don't have to do that any room is fine, it's just my daughter and myself."

"But I insist, Doctor the suite is your with my complements. You have helped my family."

Knowing that arguing would hurt the man's pride, Lori agreed. "Then we would be glad to take the suite—But I insist at paying the full price."

The clerk frowned. "No-no It will be the regular price. I insist."

It looked like Lori would have to agree. "Estan bein, okay. Does that sound good Zoe? Zoe where are you?"

"Very well, I will prepare the room for you." His fingers typed in a blur on the keyboard. The clerk finished and nodded at a porter for their luggage.

"Thank you for your effort."

Glancing around the busy lobby, Mom was in a temporary panic. Where's Zoe? Mom spun around her green eyes like a hawk looking for its prey. There is Zoe!

In the middle of the large lobby, on one knee, Zoe was kneeling and petting a dog. Of course, she's with a dog and Rosie right along beside her. Zoe absolutely love's dogs and for that matter all types of animals just like her mother.

Watching Zoe, *I guess it runs in the family.*

The dog owner, a middle age Hispanic lady and Zoe were chatting like old buddies. Rosie leaned her long collie nose forward and rubbed the other dog's shoulder, which looked like a Labrador mix.

Lori resisted getting mad, Zoe should have never left her side, especially in Mexico. Mom marched over there; "Zoe come over her—please. Let's you, me, and Rosie go to our room so we can get cleaned up and see the butterflies before it gets dark."

Turning her head, Zoe's lower lip started to pout. But Mom would have none of that pouting.

Frowning in return," Come on young lady let's get going."

"Just a moment, Mom."

Patiently, Lori stood there.

Starting to move, Zoe suddenly spun aground and gave the Labrador a goodbye hug. The dog let out a soft whine and Rosie also whine in return. Saying goodbye to the owner, Zoe returned to Mom's side.

"Okay Zoe lets get to our room."

"I agree let's go."

All kids are excited to see their hotel room for the first time.

Tugging on the leash Zoe commanded Rosie to follow. The big golden collie leaned back stretching out her front paws, like the dog was thinking about coming or staying.

Zoe gave a tug again, "Come Rosie, we're going to our room. Stay close."

Out came a short bark--okay.

"Come on Rosie, follow Zoe."

The dog tilted her head.

Receiving two key cards from the front desk clerk, Mom placed them in her handbag. The clear talked to her in Spanish for a moment and Lori answered back. Zoe only understood a little, but she was taking Spanish lesions.

Mom said, "Listos."

Nodding, Zoe that meant ready. She motioned to Rosie.

"Come Rosie—come."

Mom, Zoe and Rosie set off for the room and they were excited to see what kinda suite they were getting. Mom started to insert the keycard.

"Wait Mom, can I do it?" asked Zoe with the enthusiasm of youth.

Looking around cautiously, Mom nodded. "Sure honey, let's see what we got."

Smiling Zoe flashed the keycard. "Wait for me Rosie, but Rosie did not wait. The door opened and in bounded Rosie out racing Zoe, to scout out the room to see if it was safe. Zoe quickly follow the large canine. The clerk had definitely given them a large suite. The long hallway lead to a set of three rooms to be exact. The main room's far wall was a line of windows, the curtain's opened looking out to the ocean. The dog trotted over to the windows panting and looking out for anything to bark at. The floor had a light gray marble finish. Two ivory sofa's made a V shape with a two meter TV hanging on the wall. A pair of chairs were by a small round table with a black lamp. A kitchenette decorated the corner. On the other corner sat a large desk and bamboo chair. Tall dark gray urns and pots accented the room.

"Following behind, Lori called out, "Don't jump on the bed!"

Sprinting into one of the two bedrooms Zoe disappeared, a squeal sounded out from the doorway. The sound of someone jumping on the bed was heard. Mom started for the room to tell Zoe to stop and behave, but there was a knock on the door. Lori opened it, a porter questioned her.

"Were you want the luggage, Mum?" He boomed in a deep Jamaican accent.

Pointing to a corner the man set down the luggage. He turned and headed to the door. As he left, she gave him a generous tip. He smiled, "Tanks Mum," gave a slight bow, and left.

"Rosie, go get Zoe," the collie obediently trotted off to the bedroom.

Suddenly she heard the sounds of the dog and girl playing. Ignoring it, Lori shook her head and picked up her iPhone, she rolled through contacts and her finger's tapped the screen, an image of a sandy hair rugged handsome man nearing 40 years old appeared. The name showed an icon of Steven.

WE HAVE ARRIVED SAFE

NO THANKS TO BIRDS

………

BIRDS?

………..

FLAMINGOES

………..

WHAT!

………

MADE 4 INTERSTING LANDING

....

LANDING

....

NEAR TROUBLE WITH ENGINE

....

ARE U 2 SAFE?

....

YES

....

GOOD

....

LYB

....

BYE & BYE TO ZOE

....

Steven's image faded into a screen saver of several koala bears. Zoe came out of the room smiling and giggling, Rosie close behind.

"Was that Dad on the phone, I wanted to say hi."

"We were only texting Zoe, we can talk to the men after dinner."

"But I wanted to talk to Dad."

"Later, we can't stay long. We need to get going--now. Let quickly clean up before we go."

"But I did want to talk to Dad."

"I understand Zoe. We can talk to him later tonight."

Looking at her hands full of dog fur, "Yeah Mom, I guess I should clean up before we go. C'mon Rosie lets go."

"Great! We need to get to our car rental and get to the beach to see the butterflies." Mom opened a travel case. "The Sian Ka'an National Biosphere reserve has one of the best butterfly migrations in the world. Today we'll go there and tomorrow we can go to Talum, the ancient Mayan costal city.'

"I know Mom you already told me. We do get to bring along Rosie, right?"

"Of course, Rosie gets to go, we can't leave her behind."

Rosie barked once in agreement.

"You're the best Mom--sometimes." Said Zoe giving a funny smile.

Lori stopped and looked up from unpacking. "What ?"

"Nothing Mom. I just know Rosie want's to come with us."

"Let's get dressed and get to the beach"

Zoe did not have to be told twice, girls love butterflies and sandy beaches. From what pictures Zoe had seen Sian Ka'an is a beautiful reserve on the Yucatan Peninsula. The Lund's are looking forward to what should be a great mini vacation, but time would tell.

But you never know when you might get hit by a flamingo.

CHAPTER 2

"This road isn't that bad Mom."

"Maybe you should drive awhile, my hands and wrists are sore from holding the wheel to tight." Mom's voice sounded rough and ragged.

"You know I'm not old enough to drive, that's a few years away. But I am getting to be a good co-pilot."

"You will be Zoe, you razor sharp eyes don't miss much."

Reaching back, Zoe rubbed Rosie's long nose; "Rosie doesn't miss a thing either."

Smiling approvingly, Lori commented; "You're right, she can bark at anything from a coyote to a leaf falling."

"You're right Mom, sometimes she does barks too much."

Lori had to agree, "She's just doing her job, collies are guardian dogs." She picked up a bottle from the cup holder and drank some water.

The Lund's drove in silence for a couple of minutes bouncing up and down the Mexican state highway.

"I got a funny one Mom."

"What's that?"

"It's about Rosie's loud barking."

"What's that Zoe." Mom asked, drinking more water in the hot afternoon.

"I got a new joke, Rosie's bark is so deep it's her subwoofer."

Sipping her water, Mom about spit it out. That's funny I can't wait to tell Dad and Zac."

"But...but I want to tell them. It' my joke."

"So it is, good job young lady. The sign up ahead of us, what's is say? See if it matches my GPS."

The park sign ahead read, Reserva de la Bio'sfera Sian Ka'an.

"Yes mother, is it the Sian Ka'an national reserve. That means we are here." Zoe let out a squeal of delight. Rosie briefly whined along.

"Okay you two, calm down, I'll pull in and park."

Anxiously Zoe said, "I can't wait to see all the butterflies and the other wildlife. There are supposed to be 1000's of plants, insects, frogs, and animals. I did say butterflies, right?"

Mom agreed, "It's the most astonishing part of the Yucatan peninsula, known for its natural beauty, coastal wetlands, and shimmering lagoons. The reserve protects the fragile ecosystems and environment."

"What's an ecosystem?"

141

Lori smiled at her daughters curiosity. "A community of living organisms, like plants and animals that live in particular area."

Just made it simple, "Then they have dolphins and marine turtles in the coral reef, right?"

"That's correct Zoe."

"How about manatee's"

"Yes, what about them?"

"They are mammals, right." Zoe rapidly rubbed her hands together, "They are so cute. I remember seeing them in Florida"

"I agree they are cute. Manatees belong to a group of animals called Sirenia. There are also Dugongs who look quite alike- similar in size and shape and both have flexible flippers."

"So how do you tell them apart?" Asked Zoe.

"Great question, a manatee has broad rounded tail, and a dugong has a fluked tail or split tail like a whales."

"Let's not forget those adorable salamander's the axolotl. I had a stuffed animal one when I was eight or nine."

"That's right." Mom recalled. "You took it to bed and slept with it for about a year."

Putting a finger to her mouth and whispering. "Okay Mom, but don't tell anybody now that I'm almost a teenager."

"You're secret is safe with me."

"It better be." Zoe let out a giggle.

The two talked up a storm about marine life for a while, Zoe was always wanting to learn something new.

The battle grey Toyota RAV4 Hybrid pulled into a parking lot. Mom located a parking space, and they came to a stop.

"We are here Rosie. Ready to see some butterflies?"

Rosie woofed "yes" in agreement.

Both Lori and Zoe laughed. They got out of the SUV, Zoe opened the hatchback and Rosie bound out. She raced a lap around the vehicle whining in excitement.

Zoe called to her; "Rosie come here—now. Rosie come."

Slowly Rosie lowered her head and approached Zoe.

Bending over as Rosie licked her cheek. Zoe giggled and pushed Rosie away.

"Stop it girl. Let me put on your lead."

Rosie barked again.

"Okay Rosie let's take a walk."

The dog pulled on the lead, eager to be on her way.

"Don't go two far." Mom called out.

Mom loaded up two daypacks with water, snacks, and sunscreen. As if an afterthought, Lori placed in the pack a yellow canvas bag trimmed in black in her daypack. They put on their backpacks and adjusted them for a comfortable fit.

"Are you ready for hiking and butterflies daughter?"

"Always read for adventure Mom."

Nodding, Zoe commanded Rosie, "Hup, Hup."

The three adventurers headed out to explore the sights of the Reserve. They hiked for an hour taking in the many sights of Sian Ka'an. Constantly, Rosie was on guard for danger, an occasional growl warned them of animals, scents, and sometimes other tourists. The Lund's marched by trees, bushes, shrubbery of many various types, shapes and countless shades of green..

"Mom...I need some water.'

"Sure, no problem" said Mom, breathing normally and regular. They drank water admiring the Palm trees. "Look at that Palm tree Zoe."

Zoe eyed the tree, it looked marble like, which seemed strange to her. "I'm watching Mom."

Picking up a rock, Mom whipped it at the trunk of the tree. The tree trunk sprang to life and thousands of moths flew, flittered and scattered away into the Caribbean blue sky.

Wow!" said Zoe awed by the beauty of nature. 'How did you know to do that?"

"I'm on top of it dear, I did research on the region before when working in an Animal Hospital down here. It's hard not to be fascinated by the insects and animals here."

"That was quite a surprise, good job Mom."

"Your welcome," Mom answered, and she started hiking away.

Quickly Zoe followed and made their way to a clearing by the beach. The Gulf of America formally called the Gulf of Mexico was sending in one meter waves pounding against the sandy beach. The ocean spray reflecting the bright rays of the sun.

Stopping on point, a growl issued out of Rosie's throat. On a large boulder basking in the sun, perched an iguana, and what an iguana it was, almost three meters in length. It's tail almost making up half of its length. Strands of seaweed were dangling out of its mouth, its small but sharp teeth munching away. Rosie strained at the leash, prancing around wanting to give chase to the oversize lizard.

Straining back, Zoe pulled on the lead against the mighty muscles of the large collie. "Whoa girl, whoa."

So badly Rosie wanted the lizard, Zoe had trouble keeping the dog in control. Mom came over and firmly held the dog's long nose. "Down Rosie."

Whisking them away, Mom lead down to the beach. After thirty minutes of the sun beating down on them they stopped for another water break.

"When do we get to see the butterflies Mom?"

Shrugging her shoulders, "I guess now is as good as time as any."

"Okay. Let's go before Rosie decides to go after a jaguar."

Frowning, Mom groaned, "That might not be such a good idea. We better get going."

Thinking about it, "Your right Mom, I was just clowning around."

Consulting her cellphone for info, Lori headed northwest in quick stride. Zoe and Rosie tagged along. In about twenty minutes the terrain changed, it became wet and marshy. Wetland plants sprung up, grasses, duckweed, and ferns mixed with tall cattails flowering plants. Insects hummed and buzzed around, the sounds of frogs joined in. The Lund's followed a hiking trail that had been beaten down by human traffic. The insects, flora, and vegetation thicken along with the sounds of the insects.

Zoe's young eyes were keen, alert for movement, that is for butterfly movement to be exact.

Stopping, the youth pointed. "Mom, look over there!"

Swarms of butterflies flew about in a field of sunflower's.

"Why are all the butterflies over there?" Zoe asked.

"The Mexican sunflowers draws the most butterflies." Mom explained.

Holding Rosie tightly; "Look at the colors Mom, that swarms violet and that one is brown and the other group orange."

"You call a group of butterflies a kaleidoscope, because of all the colors."

For some reason, Rosie kept pulling at the lease.

"They sure are pretty Mom, it's amazing, there must be thousands flying around. " Zoe's voice became harsh. "Rosie-no--stop, be calm."

A low growl issued from Rosie's throat.

Staring at the spectacle, Mom said. "It's more like tens of thousands. This place is world famous for its butterflies." Mom started taking pics and video's.

Growling and straining forward, Rosie let out two sharp barks. A butterfly flew by followed by another, Rosie snapped at one, and snapped at another, the second one less fortunate lost a wing.

"Rosie!" Cried out Zoe. "Stop it! No biting."

Bending down and picking up the wounded butterfly, Zoe gently held it in her hand. Rosie lowered her head, a slight whimper sounded.

"Mom, what do I do?"

"There's not much to do but gently sit the butterfly down and see if it recovers." Mom said soothing.

Shaking off what might have been a tear, "Okay Mom. Rosie no biting."

The women followed the butterflies for a while and Mom took plenty of pictures. The two ladies giggled and laughed, Zoe took a couple of selfies and some pics of them both. After a half hour a water and snack break later, they worked their way inland. The ground turned swampy like a marsh. Growling, Rosie went on point.

Struggling holding the large collie, Zoe asked. "What Rosie, what is it? What do you see?"

Barking, and again louder, she started pulling on her lease, trying to break loose.

"Rosie, whoa! Down girl, down."

Rosie's back muscles became tense, and the hair rose on the back of her neck.

"Mom, I need help…"

Rearing back on her hind legs like a horse, Rosie's barking became more savage.

"Mom, I can't hold her."

"I'm coming Zoe."

Just as Mom was about to grab the lease, Rosie raced forward breaking loose from Zoe. Zoe screamed in pain from the lease being torn out of her hand and in fright at Rosie running away. Rosie headed for a white nosed animal that looked a lot like a racoon. The racoon creature was attacking a quail bravely trying to defend it's nest of eggs.

The Lund's started out after Rosie, but as we all know you can't outrun a dog. As they dashed after Rosie, Zoe yelled, "Mom! What is that thing?"

Being an exotic animal veterinarian, Lori yelled back. "It's Coati, a cousin to a racoon."

With the defenseless quail in its mouth now, the coati was shaking it about. The quail's squawking was of no use. While galloping fast, Rosie barked sharply, her legs poetry in motion. The coati started dragging backward the poor bird, that would become today's lunch. But Rosie would have none of that. She leaped over a fallen log and pounced—where the coati was. The racoon had dragged the bird a

149

couple of meters away by now. Rosie landed and turned to jump toward the two creatures, but Rosie stumbled and fell forward. The collie struggled to get up but couldn't. It seemed like her two rear paws were stuck like glue to the sand. The collie whinnied, much like a horse, she hopped up and down stuck in the sand.

As Zoe neared the dog; "What's wrong with Rosie?"

"I don't know." Lori slowed down as she neared the log.

The dog's head bounced up and down with short shrill barks sounding out. Lori came to a screeching halt, and Zoe partially collided into her. She leaned around Mom and peered at Rosie, her lower body sinking into wet sand.

"Mom, what is happening?"

"It's quicksand. Rosie's in quicksand!"

"Rosie, I will save you." Zoe jumped over the log to help Rosie but came to a halt. Mom's hand firmly held onto her arm and yanked her backwards. Zoe landed on a foot and a knee and struggled to get up.

"Hold on young lady, we need to think this out."

"But Mom, but Mom…She's sinking."

Over half the dog was in the quicksand, her fur coated with gooey slimy sand. Rosie's barking had diminished to whimpers, whines, and occasional barking. Zoe lowered herself to try to grab one of Rosie's paws.

"I said stop—now." Mom commanded. "I can't afford to have both of you get stuck in the sand."

Frozen by her mother's command, Zoe stopped. She knew how important it was to obey your parents you never know when it will be life or death. Lori got busy in her backpack.

The dog looked so sad, with pity in her big brown eyes. Rosie's eyes said "help me" to Zoe.

"What do we do Mom?"

"The first thing is don't panic. We need to think before we act."

Zoe looked like she was going to cry, but she didn't, she was a Lund. They were a strong and hearty family and did what needed to be done.

"Tell me what to do Mom."

Whipping out a small bag, unzipped it, Lori took out a bundle of rope. She rapidly started unwinding the nylon rope that had been in her backpack.

"Hang in there honey, I'm thinking as I go."

"We got to save Rosie—Mom we have to."

"Believe me, Zoe I know."

As if on cue, Rosie let out a pitiful howling bark, her golden fur dark and wet plastered to her skin. Lori

151

had the rope loose with the rest in a coil, it was an 8mm Rock & Rescue   rope had a small GT hook attached to the end. She swung the rope back and forth in a loose semi-circle.

"Zoe tell Rosie to bite."

"Gotcha Mom. ROSIE! Bite girl, bite!"

Letting the rope fly, Mom's toss landed about a meter short of the dogs long snout. The dog snapped it mouth and barked twice in frustration.

"Again, Mom, harder!"

Biting her lower lip, Lori dragged the rope back through the sand. She wiped off the hook and gave the rope a mighty heave. It sailed in the air and hit Rosie on the nose-ouch! The hook rolled over into the quicksand. Rosie bit at it but couldn't get a good grip. The dog sunk a few more centimeters.

"Hurray up Mom, she's sinking more, and more. What are we going to do?" wailed Zoe

"Mom, we have to save Rosie!"

"I know, I know!" Lori's hands were winding in the room, about three meters away it snagged and got stuck. "Oh, dear Lord, the rope it's stuck. Zoe come over here and help me yank it free."

"On it!"

Zoe jumped over to where Lori stood. Mother and daughter grabbed the rope and pulled, nothing happened. They wrapped the nylon rope abound
152

their hands and strained harder and harder, the rope moved a meter at best. Rosie continue to sink further into the bog.

"Okay Zoe we need to work like a team and operate together."

"But Mom, Rosie doesn't have much time."

"Zoe listen we need to be a team to save Rosie. When I count to three, on three pull like you never have pulled before."

Through teary eyes Zoe agreed; "Okay Mom—on three."

Lori found that she was almost in tears also, but she had to be strong for Zoe.

"One-two-threeee!"

The Lund's gave it their all, the hook snapped loose, and the two ladies fell backwards landing on the sand. Under different circumstances it would have been funny, but it isn't funny now. Rosie, now up to her fore paws was kicking like she was trying to swim. Her whimpering became a terrible thing to hear.

"One more try Zoe, wipe off the rope-quickly."

They wiped off the rope with their shirts becoming quite sandy and messing. Swinging the rope back and forth, Lori heaved it skyward. The hook sailed in the air in an arc and started to descend. Would it descend and land in the right place? Could Rosie have the bite and strength to hang on as Mother and daughter pull her out?

CHAPTER 3

The smartphone rang and rang, unnoticed in the excitement of the attempted rescue of Rosie.

Zoe cocked her head, "Mom, do you hear something?"

Shaking her head no, Mom coiled the rope for a finale desperate toss; "The phone is not important right now. All that matters is saving our dog, she's part of the family."

"But I'm sure I heard something Mom."

"Focus on the dog Zoe."

"Right Mom! We need to save Rosie."

Struggling against the marshy ground, which was almost up to Rosie's furry neck, the dog whimpered.

Again, the smartphone rang, then went to voice mail.

"Dad, did Mom answer?"

"No Zac it went to Mom's mailbox."

"But I wanted to tell her about my promotion in Karate."

"Son, I'm sure their having fun, probably having the time of their life in Mexico. You can tell her about it when we have our goodnight talk."

"You're right Dad we don't want to interrupt their fun adventures. Those girl's sure know how to party."

"Your right son, but something feels weird."

"I'm sure their okay Dad. Mom's a tough cookie."

Sitting the smartphone on the table at their house, Dad asked. "Want to go out and play basketball and shoot some hoops?"

"Okay Dad, we can't let Mom and Zoe have all the fun, they are probably having a picnic right now.

"Right let me get my Jordan's and some water."

"I'll get the basketball."

The two Lund men grabbed two Yeti bottles filled with water and headed outside.

Meanwhile back at Sian Ka'an Reserve, things were not a picnic—not at all. Somehow Rosie had gotten hold good bite of the rope's hook thrown to her, Mom and Zoe were pulling for dear life. The bite of an average collie was over two hundred pounds per square inch. Rosie was above average size, and highly motivated to bite and hold on for life or sink into the quicksand-forever.

Acting like a cheerleader, Zoe called out, "C'mon girl. C'mon Rosie, bite hard. Come to me Rosie. Come."

Finding herself joining in, Mom called out, "Come Rosie—come!"

Rosie's front paws came free of the sticky sand, and she gained a meter or two toward the Lund's. Lori wrapped the nylon rope around her waist digging her feet into the sand going backward. The going extremely tough for Mother Lund. Inching out on her belly, Zoe didn't notice the tearing of her shirt on the small coral rocks, she pulled with her strength on the rope. The collie kicked one rear paw free and growled as she clenched the hook with her canine teeth. Much the way a dog growls when playing tug-of-war with a stick or sock.

Only two meters away, Zoe kept coaching Rosie to keep biting and pulling with her snout.

"Rosie, you got it girl, just a little more."

"Good job Zoe, you're doing great with Rosie."

"I'm doing my best Mom."

Kicking her rear haunch legs loose, Rosie popped out of the dangerous quicksand. She released the hook and laid on top of the sand panting. Zoe reached out, rubbed sand, grit and slime from the poor dog's nose, and eyes. Rosie lay there on the sandy bank whimpering with her tongue sticking out the side of her mouth.

Zoe patted Mom on the shoulder; "Way to go Mom, you did it."

"There is no 'I' in team, we did this together. I never could have got Rosie out without your help."

Trying to smile, Zoe said, "We all did it together like a team, you, me and Rosie."

As if in answer, the dog let out a loud bark. Sand falling off their clothes, Mom and daughter hugged each other.

Later that day, back in the safety of their hotel room: "That was quite an adventure young lady, getting Rosie out alive."

"Don' forget giving her a bath was almost as tough a battle. The bathroom is a mess of sand, dog hairs, assortment of plants and twigs. Mom it will be a long time before I want to see sand again. I will only swim in swimming pools for the rest of my life. No more beaches for me."

Rosie barked in agreement.

"Slow down Zoe, it's only the start of our vacation."

Again Rosie barked.

Zoe added, "You're right Rosie, no more sand or beaches for Rosie either,"

"We will see about that Zoe, never is a long time."

The ladies laughed, but Mom knew that someday Zoe would make it back to the ocean in her lifetime. Mom checked her phone, there were several messages, notifications, and emails on it, not to mention other posts if she checked her social media.

Noticing it's past six o'clock, Mom commented, "No wonder I'm so hungry. Zoe, shower and get cleaned up and tonight we are going to order in food. It's too late to get ready and go to a restaurant. What do you want tonight, remember its VK. Whatever you want? Anything."

Brightening up; Zoe looked into her mother's sea-green eyes. "Anything? I can have anything. Okay, but I want only one thing. How about pizza…and ice cream."

Sitting the smartphone down, Mom looked at Zoe. "That's two things.

Giggling, in a girls voice, "How about Chinese?

"Now that's three things."

"Then just get me pizza and ice cream, I'll let you off the hook about having Chinese too."

"Okay, you win, we will have pizza and ice cream. We can burn off the carbs with tomorrow's hike."

"Okay, Mom."

Shaking her head, Lori mumbled, "Pizza and ice cream."

This is the kind of talk kids love to have, it drives their parents crazy. Lori has dealt with this kind of nonsense before. Zoe was smart and having lots of fun teasing her mom. Mom had to agree with Zoe's logic.

"I will order pizza and that's it."

"But Mom, you know I will be hungry later. I will be too hungry to go to bed and I am a growing girl."

"Yes you are, give me your pizza order?"

"Okay…but I will be hungry later for my bedtime snack."

Mom nodded in agreement. Glad that Zoe didn't mention ice cream. But the idea of ice cream did seem good after such a hot day.

About two hours later: They were picking up the pizza remains and putting the few surviving pieces in the mini-frig. Rosie stood there on guard in case any crumbs fell. Going to the sofa, they looked at the big monitor on the dresser and surfed through the TV menu looking for a movie. Rosie placed her paw on Zoe's thigh.

"Zoe did you feed Rosie? She looks hungry."

"Oh, sorry Mom, it has been quite a day. Can you feed her".

"She's your dog, you need too."

"Do I have to?"

Mom folded her arms.

This time Zoe knew better than to disagree. "All right be back in a minute, but I want to get a movie going."

"I'm not going anywhere."

"Then I'll get my doggie some food."

"You just do that." Said Mom trying to hide a smile.

Zoe started to speak but caught Mom's smile.

Rosie went over and pawed at her food container.

Getting the hint, Zoe sighed. "Fine let's feed you girl." Zoe gave Roise three cups of dog food into a bowl and made her shake hands and high five her before she said, "Okay."

Released Rosie eagerly ate her food, it had been a long day for her also. Watching for a moment, Zoe then went over to Mom.

"Mom, I want to watch *IF*."

"Zoe you've seen it about a dozen times."

"Okay Mom, then one more time won't hurt."

Arguing with a child is like arguing with a lawyer. Mom knew better.

"Okay, let's get the movie started. Zoe" She handed the remote to Zoe.

"Thanks, you a great mother."

"It's easy with you Zoe—sometimes."

They both giggled.

If that was all really it took, then life is good.

"Great Mom, then we get to watch the movie."

"Sure, why not?"

"I'll get is set up then."

"*IF* was a great movie and ten years later after the initial release it still held up. The movie was a family/comedy about a young girl seeing everybody's else's imaginary friend, it had some heartfelt and tender moments. For Mom, she enjoyed the great cast of actors and actresses. The movie already had started and had reached the midway mark.

"Mom, we need to stop the movie."

"Okay but tell me why?"

"Mom I'm hungry, can we stop and get some ice cream."

Mom sighed, "Pick a place to stop and we will talk about it."

"Okay." Within sixty seconds Zoe paused the show.

"Ice cream, I want ice cream."

" Young lady, where are we going to get ice cream at this time of night?"

"Hmmmm," Zoe rubbed her chin. "Let me think for a moment."

"I don't think we can get Door Dash in Mexico, or anyplace else that can deliver ice cream."

Frowned Zoe snapped her fingers, "I got it Mom."

"What's that dear."

"How about room service? This is a big Hotel. Kids stay here so they should have ice cream."

"Hey that's not a bad idea. I call down to the front desk and ask. I don't normally do ice cream, but since we're on VK. I will ask."

"Will you? Will you Mom, that would be great."

Picking up her smartphone, Mom called down to the front desk. "This is room 107, do you have ice cream available for room service?"

Listening, Mom's forehead creased. "Un hah, a hah." She listened, than a smile appeared on her face. "Mint chocolate chip. A hah." Zoe leaned closer trying to hear what was being said.

"Make it two and make both orders double scooped."

Zoe let out a small cry, "Hurray! Mom you are the best—thanks."

Giving Mom a brief hug, Zoe went over and lay on the floor next to Rosie and started petting her. Rosie stretched out her armpit so she could be rubbed deeper, both girls looked contented for the moment.

Looking at her smartwatch, the time showed 8:09. "Zoe why don't we call Dad and Zac while we're waiting on the ice cream and the movie is paused."

Laying there petting the collie. Zoe rolled on her side with the dog to scratch Rosie's furry belly.

"Get up now Zoe, we don't want the ice cream to melt when it gets here."

"Okay, let's call Dad, but I'm not sure I want to talk to Zac."

Mom tapped the call button on Steven's icon. The *Calling via Verizon* screen showed, the call rang three times, then four.

A deep warm voice answered, "Hello dear, how are my two favorite ladies?"

"We're just fine, just watching a movie and taking a break to call you. How is Zac doing?"

"He's pooped, Zac's been doing Motocross all day and he's worn out and achy from all the jumps. How Zoe?"

"She's okay laying on the hotel room floor petting Rosie. Just a great day at the Sian Ka'an Reserves, nothing but sand dunes and butterflies. We enjoyed the hike for a while…then." Lori quickly shut up.

"Did you say something Lori?"

"No, that's okay, you go ahead."

"Okay, I was going to say that I heard the butterflies kaleidoscopes are awesome."

"Yes, they are beautiful."

"Did Rosie chase a few?"

"You could say that Steven. Rosie ran around a lot."

"Mom, let me talk to Dad, give me the phone—por favor."

Handing the phone to Zoe, she put her finger to her lip sand whispered,

"Nothing about Rosie."

Zoe tilted her head, "No?"

Mom shook her head no.

"Hi Dad, how are you?"

"I'm fine honey. I miss you, are you having fun without me?"

"Sure Dad. We're going to have ice cream for the second half of *IF*. How's bro?"

"He had a rough day at the track and crashed twice."

"Is he okay, can I talk to him?"

"He is in the shower, but I'll tell him we talked, and you asked about him and said goodnight."

"But I didn't say…"

A knock sounded at the door, a muffled voice call out, "Room Service."

"Did I hear a knock?" asked Dad.

"It's okay Dad, It's the ice cream, it's here now. I gotta go, I love you guys—by. Here's Mom."

Mom took back the smartphone, "Guess we can talk longer tomorrow night. Sorry honey, can't talk anymore, room service is here." LYB. (love you by)

"No worries Lori, you two have a good night sleep. LYB."

"Say goodnight to Zac for me."

"I will –bye."

Puttin down the phone, Mom looked at Zoe. "Well?"

Frowning, Zoe looked puzzled at first. "Oh, what? Why didn't you tell Dad about Rosie almost drowning in quicksand?"

"Because he would worry, in fact he would worry about us the rest of the trip. And I don't want that. We need to have fun and so do Dad and Zac."

Thinking about that for a moment Zoe agreed, "That's pretty smart of you Mom. Can we eat ice cream and watch the rest of *IF*."

"Absolutely, we will tell Dad about Rosie and our VK when we see them in two days. That's when they fly down here to meet us."

Zoe had already started opening one of the containers. "Sounds great now, where are the spoons?"

Spoons were found, then Mom got a couple on napkins, and seats were had. The movie started to stream on the TV. The women got comfortable, the movie got started. They forgot the world and all of its problems, and enjoyed the ice cream and the movie. Afterwards, Mom and Zoe prayed and said goodnight. Zoe got into her pajama's and dragged herself into bed, it had been a long day. The rooms lights were turned off. A few minutes later, Rosie had sneaked up onto the bed matress next to Zoe, something they never would have allowed at home. Partially awake Zoe reached over and petted the dog. Her hand drifted off the dog as she fell asleep to the dog's deep breathing and panting.

For the Lund family, the rest of the night was uneventful.

Chapter 4

"Time to get up Zoe."

"Err! Leave me alone Mom. I'm going back to sleep."

"Zoe, let's get up."

"But were on VK, can't I sleep in?"

"Okay, but only thirty minutes while I make coffee and check my work emails." Mom rubbed Zoe's strawberry blonde her for a few seconds, Zoe pushed her hand away and rolled over in bed. Mom shook it off thinking waking up Zoe is about as much fun as waking up a bear. She went over and started the coffee. A few minutes passed, Rosie got up and went to the hotel door wined and placed her paw on it.

"Zoe get up the dog wants out. Zoe-get up."

Mumbling something about ice cream, Zoe sat up rubbing her eyes and stretched about on the bed, something like a cat. Finally, after a yawn, a few complaints, she got up and got dressed. Not daring to let Zoe walk the dog alone, Mother and daughter took the dog out for a short walk and a potty. The Lund's returned to the Hotel room, took a quick swim in the pool to wake up and toweled off. Afterwards they ate some granola and fruit, Mom and Zoe got dressed for the day and headed out.

"These rough roads are getting plenty bouncy Mom."

A severe bump caused the Toyota Rav-4 to swerve, Mom gripped the wheel tighter. "They sure are."

"How far to the Mayan ruins?"

Mom glanced at the GPS screen on the vehicle's center console, "Less than two hours, honey."

"That's a long time for…" Zoe glanced at Rosie. "For a dog."

"If that's your story Zoe stick to it, but we should have a talk about safety."

"What about safety Mom?"

Lori's voice changed, "We almost lost Rosie yesterday and it could have been you or me just as well. What do you know about cenotes?"

"I've heard of them, but not much."

"Not to be too technical, they are a natural pit or sinkhole caused by the collapse of limestone by water running underneath. A *cenote* is a Mayan word for ground water."

Oh—okay, and?"

Mom's tone of voice became serious. "They can be quite dangerous, we don't need trouble two days in a roll—right?"

"Let me get this straight. We should be worried about water in the ground?"

"Not exactly. The water causes the ground and limestone to collapse and makes deep large whole."

"Oh, so we don't want to fall into the holes?"

"Correct. These holes are huge and sometimes a couple of hundred feet deep. The holes have fallen trees and are like hidden lakes. The are amazing quite beautiful looking."

"So that would be quite the fall. Can we climb down them?"

"Some of them you hike down to and some people actually scuba dive in them and go to underwater caves."

"That would be only for expert divers, right Mom."

"You got that right."

Mom feeling pleased that Zoe understood the dangers of cave diving.

"I think I will stick to martial arts, dancing and gymnastics."

"Good choice Zoe."

"Let's be careful and have fun Mom."

"Right, we'll be okay and have fun, no more accidents."

Let's see what happens to the Lund family today and find out.

The Toyota bumped and hopped into a mudded and dirt area that was called a parking lot in Mexico. Mom called out loudly, "Were here at Tulum."

Frowning at the mud parking lot, Zoe said only one word, "Finally."

"It's okay most of the roads here are gravel or mud."

The two ladies got out and stretched. Zoe went around to the tailgate and out popped Rosie. She barked excitedly, prancing around ready to go. "

Wroof, wroof, wroof."

"Ready to get going Zoe?"

"Sure Mom, I want to see one of these cenote's."

"Okay, you won't be disappointed."

Pulling out the leash, Zoe commanded. "Down Rosie, no barking." Zoe rubbed the dog's thick main of hair, trying to calm done the canine. "Good girl,

172

good girl." Zoe gave her a dog biscuit, that Rosie snapped up in one bite. "Stay Rosie."

Rosie sat on her hind legs, her big brown eyes trained on Zoe.

"Whoa, Rosie." Zoe held the leash and snapped it to Rosie's collar. "Want to go on a walk?" In a high voice, Zoe called out, "Rosie want a walk?"

Leaping to her feet, Rosie started straining at the collar.

"I guess that answers you question, Zoe." Said Mom.

"It sure does…let's go."

The Lund's made their way through the parking lot and entered the awe-inspiring Mayan ruins of the ancient city of Tulum. This Mayan walled city sat low to the ground.

Zoe thought about the pictures she had seen of the towering twenty story pyramids of the mighty Tikal pyramids located in Guatemala.

"Zoe, should we do a guided tour or us girls just wander around?""

"We're fine Mom, we don't need a guide to find our way around. Rosie will keep us out of trouble."

"But who's going to keep Rosie out of trouble." said Mom.

Both girls laughed. Rosie seemed to understand them and barked softly in agreement.

Using this as a teaching moment, Mom explained that Tulum once served as a major port for region of Coba, the city itself situated on 12-meter-tall or 40 foot high cliffs that line the east coast of the Yucatán Peninsula on the Caribbean Sea. They made their way through the low buildings that were dotted with iguanas, some over a meter or two long, sunbathing and running around playing.

"Look at them Mom can I take one home as a pet. I promise I will take good care of it."

"Not today, maybe for your birthday we can talk about it."

Getting excited Zoe asked, "Really, you mean that Mom?"

"We'll see, I'll say maybe for now."

Zoe accepted that answer as they walked over to the cliffs and admired the beautiful sandy beach. The blue-green sea sending in neat 1-2 meter foamy and frothy waves.

"Muy bonitas." Said Zoe trying to learn Spanish.

"Good job Zoe, that means very pretty."

They stood there relaxing and watching the waves pound repeatedly against the sandy beaches. Rosie sat and sniffed at the different scents and smells. The wind blowing back her long dark and sable colored fur, suddenly the dog sneezed. That broke the rare moment of silence. Mother and daughter laughed.

"Zoe, before we forget, we should take some pictures to show Dad and Zac."

"Okay Mom, but Zac won't care about seeing them."

"Oh Zoe, Zac cares, but he's just a teenage boy. They don't show that they care, but he does."

Thinking about it, Zoe agreed. "I guess you're right, but boys are stupid at times."

"They are not stupid, they just react to things differently." Mom explained. "Let get some pics of the ocean, and Talum, and of course you and Rosie."

"Lets get some cute ones for Dad."

"I'm sure we will."

Pictures were taken, taken and more taken. Don't forget selfies as well. Finally, they stopped.

"How long has the city been here Mom?"

"It was the last of the Mayan cites built in somewhere in the 13-14 century, then the Spanish came."

"And then what happened?"

"The nice way of putting it," Mom paused thinking. "You could say the Spanish took over and occupied

Mexico, they ran the country differently after that. Within a seventy years the city became abandoned."

Seeming upset, Zoe asked, "Where did the Mayan's go Mom?"

Trying not to frown, Mom explained, "That's a great question. The Spanish took over the country. Most of the Mayan's left and live in Guatemala now, many near Tikal Pyramids. Okay? Now let's get back to fun facts."

"Okay Mom, sometime I'll do a report in school on the Mayans and learn a lot more."

"Things to note, over there is the temple for the *god of wind*. The city faces east for the rising sun and twice a year the sun shines exactly through a hole in the temple."

"Yeah, I heard they were amazing astronomers."

"Correct Zoe, they were so accurate their calendar is only off one day every 1000 years."

"That's amazing Mom, want to know why?"

"Sure, tell me why."

"Because they didn't have computers, how could anybody do that without computers?" Zoe giggled.

Looking puzzled, Zoe replied, "Your right how did the Mayans do that without computers."

"Look it up on your smartphone Mom."

"Great idea Zoe, why didn't I think of that."

The collie pulled on her lead, apparently Rosie wanted to get going. "Whoa Rosie, we will leave in a minute.

"It does seem impossible Zoe, that the Mayans could calculate so exactly."

"I guess you do the best with what you have."

"That's true Zoe."

Mom googled *Mayan Astronomers*. A long minute went by, Mom's eyes scanned the screen. Rosie gave a soft bark at another dog going by.

"To make this as simple as possible, since I'm a veterinarian, not an astronomer. The Mayans would get in fixed positions and track the stars as they rose and set. They would use the pyramids to understand the cyclical motions. Then they would observe the passage of the Sun directly overhead twice a year to make everything accurate and with precise calculations."

"But they didn't have computers or smartphones, Mom."

"I know dear, they used math."

"So, they used computers for math."

Mom sounded frustrated. "They didn't' have…"

Bursting out laughing Zoe enjoyed teasing Mom.

"You got me there Zoe." Both of them laughed.

The Lund's enjoyed the ruins for another hour or so, then Zoe complained about being hungry. They went back to the Rav and opened up their *Igloo* cooler. It had been loaded with fruit, sandwiches and a bag of carrots to munch on. Thinking head, Lori had called room service last night and had a meal prepared for them today. They found a table and set up lunch with iced lemonade to top it off. Zoe poured some water in a plastic bowl and brought out a couple of dog biscuits.

Casually, Zoe laid the leash on the ground, Mom didn't worry about the dog running away knowing how highly trained and obedient. The dog is. "Rosie. Time for treats."

Rosie's ears perked up and twitched.

"Sit Rosie, sit."

The large collie instantly sat.

Holding out her small hand, "Shake." The dog stuck out her left paw.

"Hi five." Rosie's right paw hit Zoe's right hand. Zoe stood up and gave her a biscuit. Which Rosie snapped up. "Good Rosie, now fist bump." Rosie tapped Zoe's knuckle twice.

Mom smiled, "That's a new one, I didn't know she could fist bump. "

Happily, Zoe smiled as she got out another doggy treat. "I taught her that one last week. Next week I'll train her to wave."

Thinking about asking how Zoe would do that, but Mom decided not to. Best to leave it between the girl and her dog. Zoe turned back to Rosie, she held up her hand, then brought her hand downward. Rosie laid on her fury belly. Zoe walked back a few meters. Rosie stayed their but she wanted to move.

"Rosie come."

The dog leaped over to Zoe and received her treat. She gobbled up the biscuit. Zoe bent over and rubbed Rosie's head and ears, brightly smiling. Then Zoe gave another dog treat to Rosie.

"I'm glad you're taking such good care of Rosie it's time to take care of yourself. Let's eat Zoe, before the flies get our food."

"Your right Mom, I got so busy with Rosie I forgot for the moment that I'm hungry. Let's eat."

Leashing up Rosie, Zoe sat down and Rosie snuggled by her feet. Just to be safe in case an animal came by Zoe placed her foot on the leash. Lunch consisted of first an apple, then Ham sandwiches, with chips, carrots and dip. Zoe accidentally on purpose let a chip or two drop, that Rosie would snapp up, at least until Mom said, "No more chips!"

Zoe hand froze, as she was about to drop another potato chip. In one smooth motion Zoe's hand circled into her mouth and the chip disappeared. They finished lunch, policed the area and picked up everything including Rosie's bowl and packed away the leftovers.

"Okay let's get going." Mom said.

Calling out, "Okay. Let's go bye, bye." Rosie responded and leaped in, Zoe closed the hatch of the Toyota.

"What do you want to do now Zoe, more sightseeing of Tulum or get in some hiking?"

"To be honest Mom, Tulum is fine, but we've seen most of it. Let's go to the jungle and check it out. I want to see some wild jungle animals, maybe I can pet a sloth or an anteater."

"Young lady you would want to pet the animals, but anteaters are dangerous. Their claws are razor sharp, but if we find a sloth we can try petting it."

"Sloths it is."

"If we find some I'll take a picture or two."

Zoe thought about the how cute the pictures would look.
"Sounds great Mom."

They got back into the Rav, got out hiking gear and two *SwissGear* Campus-ready back packs.

"I bet you have your escape rope with special hook, right Mom."

"Absolutely, I will always pack the *Rock & Rescue* rope from now on after our quicksand adventure yesterday."

"Have rope will travel right Mom?"

"That's right Zoe, grab a couple of extra water bottles and let's get going."

Rose barked in agreement and pranced around. Zoe had to struggle and tug on the lease to keep her close.

"No more quicksand for us. Right Mom?"

"I sure hope not, there should be no quicksand today."

"Good, I think I have a joke."

"You have joke Zoe?"

"Yeah." Zoe's face was puzzled as the thought. "Let me think…I got it. Here it goes Mom, I will test it out on you."

Mom stood there listening to her daughter.

"What do you call three Mexicans in quicksand?"

"I give up Zoe. What do you call three Mexicans in quicksand?"

Rosie's ears raised and were twitching like she wanted to her the joke.

Snickering, Zoe said, "Cuatro, cinco."

Laughing out loud, "That's a good one, especially for our VK."

Zoe laughed with her. "I can't wait to tell that joke to the men when they get here tomorrow. Dad and Uncle Scott should get a kick out of it. We'll see about how Zac likes it."

"Oh, don't worry honey, he'll think it's funny."

"We will see Mom. I'm ready to get hiking and then back to the pool at our hotel, and then supper and then…"

"Slow down Zoe. Let's get a hike in first."

But Zoe had already started out marching, "Rosie, hup, hup."

Rosie tail wagged back and forth and off they went with Mom in the back trying to keep up. Within fifteen minutes they had left the parking lot and were deep in the jungle. The sounds of birds and insects immediately filled the hot damp tropical air. The dense trees blocked out the sun. Sounds of Bee-tee-Wee were heard and the Lunds saw a flock of yellow breasted birds with striped black and white heads. Rosie strained on the leash and deeply barked at them.

"What are they Mom? They are beautiful."

Mom promptly answered, "They are called Great Kiskadees and their distinctive calls make a funny little song. Like in Spanish, Bien-to-veo.

"I know what that means, 'I see you well.' That kinda funny and cool since I'm learning Spanish. But I really want to see a Sloth."

"Maybe Zoe, but I can't promise you that will happen."

"One can hope—right?"

A fly landed on Zoe's hand, she slapped it, squashed it, flicked it off and kept walking. Mom didn't say a word, but she was impressed by her daughter. They marched for about another thirty minutes.

Glancing at a sign on the trail Mom pointed. "This way to a cenote."

"Those are giant sink holes right Mom?"

"That's right, they are giant holes in the ground carved out over a million years by water. The word cenote come from the Mayan's which means hole with water."

Withing five minutes they stopped. Before them appeared a large hole half surrounded by trees with a pool of bluish-green water at the bottom that sparkled in the beams of sunlight. Over a dozen people were taking pictures, admiring it's limestone walls and cave formations at the bottom of the hole.

Rosie kept moving back and forth causing Zoe to have a rough time controlling the large dog.

"Tell you what Zoe my Google map on my watch says there is another cenote a bit farther on, where there will probably be less people. We can take some pictures, and we can relax and let Rosie run around some. Let's go there."

Nodding, Zoe did not have to be told twice this time. "Okay! Let's go Mom. Rosie—hup, hup."

"Don't get to far ahead." Lori called out as mothers do.

Off they went deeper into the jungle for more adventure. About forty minutes later, Lori and Zoe saw an opening in the thick brush and trees. They marched into the clearing huffy and puffing, sweat on their faces and back.

"This heat is crazy Mom, my sweat has sweat. I can't wait to get back to the pool and go swimming."

"Okay a break it is." Taking off her SwissGear backpack, Mom set it down and opened it. She took out a small plastic bowl."

"But not too long of a break."

"It will be quite a while Zoe. We have to hike back to the Toyota and then drive almost two hours to get back to the Hotel. We will see if we have time for a swim before dinner."

"I need a swim after this hike."
184

Opening a water bottle, Mom poured water into it, Rosie went over and rapidly started lapping up the water.

"We will do the best we can."

"But Mom I want to go swimming."

"Don't ruin the moment Zoe. Let's have some fun we don't have to stay too long."

"Oh—okay Mom."

Zoe let Rosie off her leash and the dog lifted its nose and sniffed in all directions then she trotted off wandering around. Zoe and Mom moved closer to the edge of the hole to look down. Zoe kicked a stone, it fell downward making a nice splash in the pool's glittering water. The ripples of water raced to the edge striking the limestone bedrock.

"Look down there Mom at the water."

"Okay, I'm coming."

Lori went closer to the edge to see the rippling water. The ground suddenly gave way, gravel and dirt fell into the cenote and Mom fell downward with the loose ground.

"Zoooeeee! Help!"

Zoe went to rim of the cenote ignoring the dangerous edge. Frightened at what she saw, Zoe screamed. "Mooooom!!!

CHAPTER 5

Eyes widened in terror Zoe stared at the sight below. Spread-eagled on a ledge beneath lay Lori. "Mom!" Zoe gasped and screamed at the top of her lungs. "Moooom! Wake up!"

Her mother's still form lay on the rocky edge unconscious! Zoe tried to regain her wits, panicking would not help. Whispering out loud, Zoe said, "Thank God for the ledge."

A fall to the bottom would of killed Mom for sure.

Squinting her eyes, Zoe tried guessing the distance, from the ledge to the bottom it must be 50 or 60 meters or over 170 feet to the bottom, with a hard rock landing. The ledge with Mom only lay about a dozen meters below, but in some ways it might as well have been over a kilometer, about a mile out of reach. Rosie whined, she went over to Zoe and nudged her hand with her nose. Zoe tried to fight back tears, Mom could even be dead. She truly didn't know if her mother was alive or not.

Calling out again and again, but Lori did not answer. She just laid there like a thrown away broken doll. Buring her head in her hands, Zoe cried. It got worse, she remembered that Mom had the only smartphone and Zoe had no way of calling for help. Should she dare leave her lying Mom there and run back to the last cenote to get help. Could Mom last that long down there if she was still alive.? What should she do?

Racing around in a circle, Rosie whimpered sat on her haunches and barked once. She then pranced over to Lori's *SwissGear* backpack and placed a paw on it and started scratching it.

"What are you doing Rosie? What are you doing with Mom's backpack?"

Cocking her head to the side, Rosie barked. The collie went to the edge of the cenote and back to the backpack and pawed it again.

Trying to quite crying, Zoe looked puzzled. "What are you saying girl? What about Mom's backpack?"

Barking once, Rosie went back to the edge of the cenote and then bounced back to the backpack. This time Rosie using her long nose, pushed at the flap on top of the backpack and barked twice. The large canine stopped and looked at Zoe tilting it's head side to side.

A light bulb turned on inside Zoe's head.

Its what's in the backpack?

What did Rosie want her to do? Through blurred teary eyes Zoe started yanking out items. Out of the backpack came flying water bottles, suntan spray, insect repellent, a pack of flares, a flashlight, large knife and the Rock and Rescue rope. As the items hit

188

the ground, Zoe searched around further and pulled out a pair of sunglasses.

In her grief she held up the sunglasses the sunlight reflecting off the lenses. Saying out loud. "What good are these?"

Barking sharply, Rosie nudged the coil of rope, she picked it up with her mouth and deposited it at Zoe's feet. Another sharp bark followed.

Slapping the top of her head, "What an idiot, I am. I'm so upset that I tossed out the rescue rope. Thanks Rosie." She hugged the dog's neck briskly.

Picking up the nylon rope and GT hook, Zoe gingerly made her way to the ledge of the cenote. Careful that she would not be the next victim and fall to her doom or even to her death. Who would save Mom then? Unwinding the rope, Zoe lowered it to the fallen figure of her beloved mother.

Slowly, slowly the nylon rope lowered, it snaked closer to Lori. Closer and closer, but abruptly it stopped a few meters short of Mom's fallen body.

"Mom? Mom, wake up. Are you alive?" That thought made another couple of tears form in Zoe's eyes.

Carefully Zoe backed away from the dangerous ledge. "Do we run and get help Rosie?"

Rosie's responded by sitting down.

189

Lifting her hands, Zoe pleaded with the intelligent dog. "We stay here and do…what?"

Tilting her head back toward the ledge, Zoe rushed over in a panic and hugged Rosie' thick main of hair. She broke out crying and sobbing. The dog's breathing deepened in worry .

"Oh God, please save my mother. She has too much work to do, to many animals to help and she needs to raise me and my brother Zac." Sob, sob, sob. "Please help us."

Zoe heard a sound, maybe a voice.

Does God talk to people?

There she heard the sound again. She strained her ears listening. The dog leaped to her feet, trotted to the edge of the cenote, and gave a soft murmuring. Rosie pranced back and forth looking downward. She stopped to bark at Zoe, but Zoe already stood there looking   downward.

"Zoe…Zoe is that you? Are you okay?"

"Mom, that's silly. Of course I'm okay. You're the one Rosie and I are worried about. Zoe's foot moved about, and a shower of dirt and sand fell.

Rosie barked in agreement. Zoe tapped the dog's flat head to reassure them both. Climbing to her feet, Lori brushed off dirt, sand and a few leaves mixed in. Peering upward, her eyes narrowed at the sight of the Rock & Rescue nylon rope. It dangled 3-4 meters overhead, it might as well be a kilometer away.

"Is that as much rope as we have Zoe?"

"I'm sorry Mom, it's all the rope we have. What are we going to do? Do you want me to go for help?"

Lori pulled back her messed up strawberry blond hair, working out some of the dirt and grit. Thinking out loud she said, "I don't know? How long have I been unconscious?" Guessing, "Less than half an hour." She called up to Zoe. "Let's think this out, for a moment before we dash off for help."

Deep inside, Mom did not want Zoe to leave and be left alone, For Zoe there were too many dangers and too many strangers. As if sensing what Mom was thinking, Zoe said, "I'll be okay to go get help, Rosie is with me. Mom, can we go? I will be back in a flash."

Shaking her head no, "In the jungle we need to stay together.. or at least try to. We need to find a way to make the rope longer or…"

Zoe jumped in, "Mom, what if we tied something to the rope?"

"Like an extension? That a great idea Zoe, but what can we use?"

"How about shoelaces, Mom?"

"Zoe, they won't be long enough or strong enough,"

"How about Rosie's lead?"

"Mom considered it, then looking at the distance between her and the hook of the rope, "It's a great idea honey, but again it won't be long enough. We need another rope or something like it."

Clapping her hands together. "I got it Mom, I have a great idea."
"What's that? Tell me." Lori asked excited by Zoe's enthusiasm.

"I go get a vine in the jungle, tie it to the rope and you climb up while Rosie and I pull on the rope-vine."

Mom rubber her dirty chin, "That just might work, but you have to promise to stay close to this area. Promise?"

"Yeah sure Mom, I won't wander off too far." Zoe gave a thumbs up. And remember I'll have Rosie with me." Zoe patted Rosie on her furry back. Rosie barked once in agreement. "We'll be right back."

"ZOE!"

Zoe paused and looked over the bank down at her Mom who looked lonely on the ledge. "What Mom?"

"Two things, one is that I love you."

"I love you too Mom. And what's the other?"

"Grab the knife out of my backpack to cut the vine."

192

"Knife?" Zoe half joked and half lied. "That's the first thing I grabbed when I opened the backpack. I wouldn't forget the knife Mom."

"Yeah right," said Mom skeptically.

"LYB."

Grabbing the Mossy Oak Survival knife, Zoe ran off with Rosie before Mom could say another word. They ran about a hundred meters and Zoe slammed on the brakes seeing vines hanging from a group of trees. Barking excitedly, Rosie pranced around Zoe. The vines all looked alike to Zoe, were some stronger than others and how could she tell. Which is the thickest vine the strongest and the sturdiest? Rosie kept prancing around Zoe. Is there something else wrong Zoe wondered?

Trying to ignore the dog, Zoe remembered an old nursey rhyme, but she changed it. "Eenie, meenie, miney mo, which vine has to go. If I pick a vine today will it get my Mother away. Eenie, meenie, miney, mo, look out vine here we go."

Grabby a green vine, Zoe pulled on it firmly and prepared to cut it. The green vine moved, Zoe received a big surprise that the vine was alive! The vine being a SNAKE! The vine snake withered and squirmed in her hand.

Eck!

Zoe let go like it like she held a hot potato. The snake detached itself from the tree, landing on the jungle undergrowth and coiled itself up getting ready to strike. Looking at the grooved fangs below the eyes made Zoe think, her Mom had taught her about snakes. Somewhere in the back of Zoe's mind she remembered that poisonous snakes have slit-like cat eyes. Rosie crouched down and growled at the unwanted snake. The snake hissed back at Rosie, it long wicked tongue flicking back and forth. The snake's head coiled back to strike. Frozen in terror, Zoe didn't know what to do.

It suddenly dawned on her that she had a knife, could she time it just right to cut off the snake's green head? Zoe moved the Mossy Oak knife blade around looking for an opening to attack. The snakes eyes following the shiny blade. The good news is that it created a distraction for her collie, that's what Rosie needed. Growling, barred her white fangs and lunged at the snake, savagely biting it just below the head. The snake rapidly coiled and uncoiled it's long meter and half body and tried to wrap itself around the collie. Rosie furiously shaking her head around, the snake fighting to get loose. The dog growling and savagely biting harder and harder. The snake's tail striking at Rosie's furry body.

The twitching tail slowed down, the snake stopped and went still, Rosie continued to growl, salvia dripping from her teeth and biting at it.

Suddenly the snake coiled and wound it's tail around Rosie's neck   tightening it. At first Rosie growled louder, then she started to whine as the snake tightened its grip.

A scream brook out, then Zoe yelled, "Leave my dog alone. Stop now."

But the snake had no intention of stopping, Zoe stabbed at it with her knife…and missed!

A scream for help came out of Zoe's mouth, but the jungle sucked up her scream in a midst of insects and bird noises. Rosie whined more, who would win the vine snake or the collie?

Summing up her courage, Zoe fought the urge to run away. But she couldn't leave her beloved dog and companion. She changed the position of the knife blade to try to again stab at the head of the vine snake. Her heart rose to her mouth, she had never been so scared in her life. She needed to save her beloved dog, Rosie.

Dancing around, Zoe looked for an opening, the collie and the snake were doing their own deadly dance. Zoe needed the right opportunity to strike. Seconds seemed like minutes as Zoe searched for an opening. The snake tightened its grip, the collie whined, growled and shook her head harder. She raised her hand with the knife to strike, her hand started whipped downward at her intended target, the snake's flat green head.

What if I hit my dog?

The fight before her gave the answer. The snake head went limp, the once vicious mouth with fangs opened, and tongue dangled out.

Rosie had done it, she had saved the day!

With a mighty fling Rosie shook loose from the once coiled snake. Its body landing on the green jungle plants. A brown and tan hawk swooped down, snatched the dead snake remains and flew away.

Standing there, Zoe was stunned by the turn of events. She snapped out of it as the hawk flew away with its dinner disappearing among the trees.

"Rosie, you did it! You got the snake, good girl— good girl." Zoe hugged Rosie so hard the dog whimpered for a moment. Finally, Zoe broke away from the canine and stood up. She brushed away a few remaining tears and let out a deep sigh.

"We have to cut a vine and save Mom." Zoe hesitantly looked at the vines, which ones were real, and which ones could be another snake… or even something worse. Bravely she reached out and touched the vine with the blade of the knife and then jumped back. The vine did not move.

Oh, thank God.

She grabbed it and started cutting it in a saw-like fashion. Within a minute or so she had procured a long length of vine. Zoe could only hope it would be

196

long enough to reach the ledge that her mother stood on.

Yelling, "Hup, hup!" She and the dog raced through the jungle to get to her Mom. It seemed to Zoe that they had been gone a long time and she didn't want her mother to worry more. At first the dash seemed endless, but before she knew it Zoe and Rosie were back at the cenote. Feeling sweat on her face and running down the back of her shirt, Zoe stopped gasping for breath in the thick humid air of the jungle. Now, Zoe heard her mother calling out.

"Zoe! Where are you? Zoe? Zoe?"

"I'm here Mom. Rosie and I are here, and we have a vine to attach to the rescue rope."

The rescue rope had been put to good use this trip with saving Rosie yesterday and would be used today to save Mom or so we hope. Zoe tied a bowline knot connecting the rope and the vine. Just like her dad, Steven the forest ranger had taught her. Scurrying to the edge, Zoe glanced down. A few more pieces of dirt and sand fell down landing on Mom.

"Hey, you're getting me dirty Zoe."

That caught Zoe off guard, and she giggled. "It's okay Mom you can have a nice shower when we get back to the room. I'm lowering the rope right now."

"Okay I can see it coming down. Zoe you did tie the rope to something—right?"

"Awwh sure…Mom."

Pulling up the rope, Zoe looked around till she noticed a convenient tree trunk nearby. Quickly she looped the vine around twice, tied a slip knot, went back to the ledge and tossed the coil of rope and vine down towards Mom. Mom's arms stretched out and barely caught it before it went off the limestone ledge.

"Is it secure Zoe?"

"I sure hope so Mom, start climbing, Rosie and I will start pulling."

"Okay, I'm ready. Start pulling Zoe!"

"We will!"

Grabbing the hook of the rope, Lori started scampering up the limestone cliff. The girl and her dog started, Rosie pulling with her teeth and Zoe pulling with her hands. The going was tough and hard. Constantly when Lori's feet struck the wall off flicked bits of the cliff giving way to the loose soil and soft limestone pebbles raining on the ledge below.

About halfway up the climb, sweat dotted Lori's forehead, her breathing ruff and ragged. She yelled, "I…I need to rest a minute—stop."

"Sure, Mom," Zoe glanced at the vine and winced. *Oh no!* It had started to dry out and split bearing Mom's weight.

198

Would it last till Mom reached the top?

"Mom get going, the vine doesn't look good. Rosie and I will pull as hard as we can. Pull Rosie!"

The dog responded with a growl and Zoe with a grunt. Her hands were now sweating from the tropical heat and damp humidity.

"Okay," Lori cried out.

Up she went agonizing meter by meter, the rim of the cliff started to look closer. Zoe frowned as another tear in the vine appeared. Would Mom make it? Another fall, Mom might miss the ledge and fall to her DOOM!

Working her along the vine, Zoe got closer to the dangerous ledge. Zoe wanted to grab Mom's hand and pull her up but had to wait for a few more meters. By now Mom had almost reached the top. The vine split again, it tore further almost pulling apart by now. Rapidly, Zoe moved her way up to the safer nylon rope trying to maintain her grip.

Zoe whistled and called out. "Rosie let go, let's go- -come here girl. You can do it. Bite again."

Somehow the amazing collie understood, let go of the vine and bit the rope in front of Zoe's right hand. The vine behind them tore apart into shreds! Instantly Zoe felt all the weight of Mom on the rope. The rope slid through her hands causing a rope burn. Gritting her teeth Zoe regained her grip. She would not let go no matter what. Her Mom's life lay in her small young hands. Zoe wished Zac stood here beside her now, for he had almost the strength of a full grown man. But he wasn't, it totally depended on her and Rosie now.

A hand appeared on the ledge, it moved around and grabbed a small bush. Then another hand appeared, the fingernails scraping at the soil. Dropping the nylon rope, Zoe plopped on her belly and wormed her way forward. Zoe grasped at her mother's hand. The Lund's two hands intertwined, love and strength flowed as only a mother and daughter could. With a mighty yank Mom landed on the top of the cenote, panting and gasping for breath in the hot jungle air. Both ladies were drenched in sweat from the mighty battle of the climb, even Rosie's fur was damp and lathered like a horse after a long ride.

The Lund's had succeeded against the cenote and Mother Nature!

They hugged like they had never hugged before, the tears flowed, no words were said or needed to be said. Finally, they pulled apart, sat down and each guzzled a water bottle, Zoe poured water in a leaf several times and Rosie eagerly lapped it up.

"What a close call Zoe. You're my hero."

"Anytime Mom." Unlike most kids, Zoe said nothing about the vine snake that story could be told in the safety of the Hotel room tonight.

"You did a great job of staying levelheaded and that was great thinking of adding that vine."

At the thought of the vine Zoe shuddered. "Let's go Mom, I want a swim and a shower and then a whole lot of food."

"You don't have to say that twice. Let's go we still have a hike to get back to the Toyota and then a quite drive back to Capybara Hotel. Let's get out a sandwich and eat it while we hike back."

Agreeing, Zoe got out two sandwiches from her backpack and they ate on the way. They mostly made small talk and tried to ignore the scary fall and rescue that had just happened. They were too shaken up for the moment. But they didn't get far before…

Roar!

Another terrible growl and grunting sounded out to their left. In a low laying forked branch in a tree perched a jaguar. He crouched there on a pile of vines in the tree like the King of the Jungle. He growled again, it sounded like the sawing of wood.

Barking like crazy, Rosie moved between the Lund's and the King of the Jungle. Fearfully, Lori and Zoe crouched behind the dog. The jaguar growled again and roared! In spite of the tropical heat chills went up Zoe's spine.

What were they going to do?

CHAPTER 6

Continually, Rosie barked and growled ferociously at the jaguar. The King tilted his head at the canine, trying to figure out the dog that challenged him. It's golden-reddish eyes gleaming in the low light of the jungle. Hissing at Rosie the great cat rose to its rear haunch's.

Holding out her hand, Mom commanded, "Zoe stay close and don't let Rosie loose. She won't win a fight against a jaguar, no dog will. If we keep back we may be able to get out of this mess."

Dropping her backpack on a mossy stone, Lori located and picked up a long stick. She proceeded to hand it to Zoe. Who grabbed the stick and with the other hand grabbed the collie's collar. She knew she couldn't stop Rosie if Rosie wanted to get free, but she could partially control her. Dr Lori had taught her children many lessons about animals.

"Look Mom, that's the problem."

A young jaguar cub ran about below the King, toying with a bird playfully.

Venturing a guess, Zoe said, "Mom must be out hunting, and Dad is guarding the cub."

"Good job honey I bet your right. Just leave the cub alone."

"But it's so cute, I want to hold it and pet it."

"Zoe no!"

"Just joking Mom, but under different circumstances I would."

"Somehow I believe you Zoe—you would."

Swiftly Lori opened her backpack and searched through it. She pulled out a plastic package, inside were several long orange sticks. The King elegantly leaped off the fork in the tree and landed by the cub, its' fur orangish in color and the black spots called "rosettes" dancing about on top of the great cat's lean sinewy muscles. The cub ignored everybody, it pawed at the bird toying with it, like playing with your food before dinner. The King head darted back and forth hissing and baring its cream colored fangs.

Standing still, Zoe knew better than to run. "Mom what are we going to do."

"I'm on it Zoe." Mom opened the package and took an orange long stick much like a candle in shape.

To make matters worse, the cub devoured the small bird, a few feathers scattered about and drifted to the floormat of the jungle. The cat started toward them, like it didn't have a care in the world and maybe it didn't. Since it's mom and dad were the top predators in the jungle, but the King cared and issued a loud growl that could be heard a kilometer away. Several birds screeched in terror and took flight from nearby tree branches. A few feathers fell, they drifted in spirals to the grassy ground. Of all things, a startled sleeping sloth in a tree branch fell to the ground, it lay there still hoping to be ignored.

The King deciding that he would chase off these intruders in his jungle, his domain. Crouching the jaguar prepared to leap at the collie. Sensing the oncoming attack, Rosie braced herself. Mom stepped into action and twisted off the cap her orange stick. Next she pushed the ignitor button. It's magnesium tip hissed and sputtered into existence. Holding the flare out horizontally in her hand away from the flaming hot slag end, Lori advanced. Waving her arm back and forth yelling as she went. The once mighty King growled but shied away from the flames. It cringed from the searing heat of the magnesium. The great cat nudged the cub harshly pushing it into the foliage and bushes. The King and his cub stood at the edge of the trail. The King gave a final roar of contempt, and the two cats disappeared, blending into the thick jungle growth.

Waving the flare about a few more times, Lori then placed it on a large boulder. Where is sizzled and sputtered. Zoe nodded her head in approval at her amazing mother. Wow! Impressed by her mother, Zoe thought maybe she would be an veterinarian when she grew up.

After the harrowing event, Mom and daughter were able to find the return path to the parking lot at Talum.

The sun and awful heat of the day their worst enemies on the hike. On the way Zoe spied on a herd of capybaras playing about. There were about two dozen or so, two or three of them were pups. Several were over a meter long, their short brown hair reflecting the sunlight. One of them even had a bird sitting on it which Zoe found to be quite funny.

"Mom, those capybaras are so cute, with their blunt snout and short front legs. Can we take one of them home? I am sure Rosie won't mind."

"No, my dear, they are illegal in most states or at least you need to have a permit. I wonder how they got here? Normally they live in South America. They must have been once been pets then they got loose and multiplied."

"I still want to take one home."

Patting Zoe on the shoulder Mom said, "Of course you do Zoe."

Mom continued on the trial, Zoe had no choice except to follow. She gave a faint wistful glance over her shoulder at the bird which stood on the back of the thick bellied rodent.

Miserably they hiked, the Lund's were sweaty and their clothes completely damp by the time they had reached the Toyota. Rosie's fur looked wet enough like she had gone swimming. Mom and Zoe toweled off some and towel rubbed Rosie. It made her fur look ratted and tangled, especially her tail feathers.

"That must have been the hike of a lifetime for us Zoe."

"That's for sure Mom, it made the quicksand adventure, seem like a walk in the park. I want to go back and get cleaned up, a girl can only handle so much adventure."

Mom drained the rest of a water bottle. "Maybe you can imagine some the wild misadventure's that your Uncle Scott has."

"You're right Mom, being a border agent has to be exciting--and dangerous too." Zoe picked up her water bottle and then took a couple of sips. "Not everybody gets to save the President of the United States."

Switching gears, Lori added, "Your Father Steven's job is important also. Being a Forest Ranger has it's thrills with poachers, illegal trappers and remember that time he caught that escape prisoner in Yellowstone National Park."

Shaking her head in agreement, Zoe remembered at that time she had been quite worried about Dad. Interrupting her thoughts her stomach growled. "Let's get to the room and have a snack. I need food after this hot mess today."

Mom couldn't argue with that. "Okay, let's get out of here. We still have quite a drive back to the hotel and I hear there's supposed to be a severe storm tonight."

"Okay Mom get it in gear and let's get back. You know how much our family loves thunderstorms and snowstorms. We can watch it from our hotel window."

Mom agreed, "That sound's great, we can watch the storm from the safety and security of our room.

"With popcorn?"

"Of course we can have popcorn Zoe."

Putting the Toyota in gear, Lori backed out of the parking spot. She shifted into drive and away they went. The memory of Talum was behind them. They were sure to talk about the incident at the cenote, snake and jaguar tonight again and again. It was tough for Zoe to keep quiet, she could hardly wait to tell her mom the story about the vine snake. In fact, it seemed like a miracle that she had not opened her mouth about it already. You know how hard it is for kids to keep a secret, much less not to constantly interrupt their parents when they are talking. Zoe knew Mom would be impressed that she had kept the secret for so long.

The ride back to the hotel room went eventful. The worst thing was the constant hunger in their bellies, they had run out of sandwiches and snacks a long time ago. The sight of the Capybara Hotel seemed a welcome sight to the tired and battered Lund's.

Both mother and daughter couldn't wait to take a quick dip in the pool and wash the stink and feel of the jungle away. Normally she loved all animals and even reptiles, but a battle between her, Rosie, and a vine snake made the story a different matter. They returned to the Hotel and quickly changed. After the refreshing swim the Lund's headed back to their room. Mom opened the hotel door, they heard the sound of snoring, there beside the bed lay Rosie taking a well needed nap.

"Mom, Rosie looks so cute and adorable."

Hearing her name, the collie sprung to her feet with a welcoming bark and raced to Zoe, like she hadn't seen Zoe for days. Zoe patted her on the head and briskly rubbed her ears.

"Head for the shower Zoe, I'm going to order dinner, I'm too tired to drive to a restaurant."

"But Mom, I wanted to go out and eat." Cried out Zoe standing there with water dripping off her swimsuit."

"I'm not going to argue. I will make it up to you. Get in the shower before you drip all over the place."

"Mom, I wanted to go out for Chinese tonight. Pleeeease!" she held her hands together in prayer position.

"I'm sorry Zoe. I'm wiped I just avoided a near fatal fall. What else can I do?" Mom held out her hands, they were rubbed raw and chaffed from climbing out of the Cenote sinkhole.

"Oh, Mom I'm sorry. I didn't know your hands were so bad. You never complained about them."

Lightly touched one hand against the other, Mom calmly said. "It's okay, they will be fine tomorrow."

Feeling bad about wanting to go out for dinner, Zoe agreed. "Let's order Chinese with fortune cookies and a movie. Okay?"

"Sure, honey lets live it up and have shrimp and sizzling scallops."

"Don't forget the noodles and lots of them for leftovers." Zoe said excitedly. "…and extra fortune cookies."

"Okay, okay, go young lady. Get in the shower now!" Zoe giggled as she pranced off to the shower, drops of water flying all over the carpet.

"Wow, the shrimp tasted great Mom."

"I think the sizzling scallops were also amazing." Said Mom finishing a bite.

"Can I open a fortune cookie now? Can I?"

"Sure honey, let's see what we get?"

Grabbing a cookie for Mom and two for herself. Mom gave her the look, it froze Zoe in place--then nodded okay. Zoe broke a cookie in two, tossing half of it in her mouth.

"Mom, here's my fortune.

If you eat something and nobody sees you eat it. It has no calories."

Mom laughed, "That's a good one. Okay, here's mine.

Help I'm a prisoner in a fortune cookie factory."

Zoe wrinkled her face, it bunched up her freckles. "It doesn't say that…does it?"

Mom sighed, "Okay…I must confess that I made that up."

"What does it say Mom?"

"If a man crosses the ocean twice without taking a bath, is known as a dirty double crosser."

Pondering that for a moment, Zoe got it and laughed, which made Lori join in. "That's funny Mom."

"Because I will open the second one…"

The sound of thunder interrupted that action. Another flash showed through the hotel window blinds. Rosie growled, went over and lay down by Zoe's feet. Zoe petted the dog reassuringly. Rosie looked up and let out a small whine. Picking up her cellphone, Mom looked at the weather app.

"Are we okay Mom?"

"I'm not so sure. It looks like a serious tropical storm."

Suddenly Mom's phone chimed with a weather alert, but Mom said nothing. Zoe went to the window and peered out. A lightning bolt interrupted the darkness of the night, the boom of thunder almost immediately following. The hotel lights flashed off and on.

Crowding closer to her mother, Zoe asked. "Are we in trouble?"

A WEA text message appeared on Lori's phone. Zoe scanned the message.

"What is a WEA?"

"It stands for Wireless Emergency Alert, it has upgraded the storm to possible hurricane force winds."

"Are we safe? What about our windows?"

Two more sparks of bright lightning went zipping across the sky that resembled fireworks. The hotel room flashed like a strobe light, thunder roared like two cracks of a mighty whip. The window's rattled, the vibration raced across the floor. Rosie leaped to her feet and crowded against them.

Putting her arm around Zoe in an attempt to comfort her, Mom said. "The windows should be safety glass. They are high impact windows and double paneled with a thin plastic membrane. We should be okay."

Taking in the magnificence and splendor of the storm, Zoe said, "If you say so Mom, but the storm does look sick."

Hearing that comment made Mom glad to know that Zoe is doing okay. She said, "Nature is violent, yet beautiful at times. I'm glad the storm didn't come early today. That would have been big time trouble if we were still out in the jungle."

Another jagged light strike sizzled outside to accentuated Mom's point. The thunder massive boom rattled the window almost immediately. The howl of the wind rose, roaring like a train, the raindrops pelted at the window. The two Lund's instantly clutched each other.

In spite of herself Mom's words were shaky. "I know it's safe, but I think we should get away from the window and go to the bathroom."

Not having to be told twice, Zoe headed to the bathroom. "Come Rosie—come."

The dog trotted obediently after them. They entered the bathroom, a refuge of safety, they hoped.

"I want to get some water, Mom. I'll get two water bottles for us, it will only take a moment."

"Okay, but hurray up." Mom stood grasping the door firmly.

I'll be as fast as I can."

"Please hurry!"

The wind howled louder, another thunder boomed. It seemed like the storm was just warming up.

The window brightly lit up like a Christmas tree from the next bolt of lightning and then the grandfather of all thunder sounded. A window shattered like dropping a plate from a great height. The wind rushed in sending the glass in a thousand splinters, the blinds rattled and came apart. Squatting, Zoe was bending overreaching into the minifridge when the blast struck. The gusts of wind blew sideways across the floor, sliding into the wall.

Mom screamed, "ZOE!"

Zoe did not answer, she lay on the floor in a crumpled heap.

Mom yelled at Zoe again, but the sound of the storm overtook her desperate cry to Zoe. She laid there the wind blowing and whipping her hair about, Lori screamed, "Zoeeeee!"

Zoe did not answer.

CHAPTER 7

The wind battled Lori as she gripped the door with all her might. The water plastered her face and hair, making breathing harsh and difficult. In the back of her mind, she knew she should get back in the bathroom and wait for rescue. Shaking her drenched head, but she could not do that. What if the rescue did not come in time, then what? Her mother instincts would never allow it. Her safety did not matter, Zoe is what mattered. Her mind became determined. Somehow she must get to her daughter.

But How?

Entering the hotel room the gust of the storm exploded, rain drops pounding at Lori, like Nerf bullets pinging her. The raging of the storm forced her to close her eyes. Blinded, Lori called out "Zoe" at the top of her lungs. She couldn't her an answer. Lori screamed "Zoe" again and again. The wind howled, the floor and door vibrated from the booming thunder. The remaining blinds broke off and skidded across the floor to the fall wall, forcing Lori to jump over them. The dog! she would call the dog.

"Rosie! Here Rosie!"

A bark sounding distant in the storm answered her.

"Rosie! Come here Rosie!"

Lowering her left hand, with the other clutching at the door for dear life. Lori's left hand fumbled about, then it found…fur. Lori grabbed the fur, working her way up to the long hair of the main, then her hand moved to the collar, and she heard a bark over the gale force of the storm.

"Rosie find Zoe. Go find Zoe! Now!"

"Wroof!

Straining the dog crept forward into the nasty storm that had invaded the room, Lori blindly followed the canine firmly grasping onto the large dog's collar. Lori's heart leaped to her throat, a prickling chill went up her spine. Could she make it to Zoe and pull her back to the bathroom. Was the bathroom even safe? Maybe they had better head out of the room to the corridor. Every meter gained seemed like forever as Lori and Rosie fought the elements of the fierce storm.

Striking an object, Lori's feet nearly tripped, a chair had blown over. She felt the tilted chair as the mother and dog moved around it. Lori could feel, more than hear Rosie growl.

Twice more, Lori called out "Zoe."

No answer sounded that she could tell. The dog pulled her forward through the sheets of water. She fumbled about on the wet carpet trying to walk. Her hand almost slipped off the wet collar. Lori regained her grip, and the dog crept forward it's claws digging into the floors carpet. Stubbornly Lori kept her grip, a grip for life. Daring to open her eyes, the spraying water making Lori's eyes were mere slits to look out through.

Lori wondered, *Can Rosie get me to Zoe?*

A blast of wind threw Lori on her knees, yet she somehow held onto Rosie's collar. It's amazing the strength a mother has when a child is in danger. Rosie growled, Lori felt it come from the collies throat then heard it.

Are we close to my child?

Something hit Lori's back, a bush, an object or a tree branch. Lori couldn't tell and didn't care, she had to make it to Zoe. At all costs!

"Rosie—get Zoe."

But She wasn't even sure it the dog could hear her. The dog stopped? Lori could feel the collar lower, she got down on her knees and searched the floor with her left hand. Her hand patted around the carpet. Finally, she found a foot, she clutched at it like she had found treasure. Her hand worked its way up the calve to the knee. Lori found herself cried, her tears mixing in with the raindrops.

217

"Zoe is that you!?!"

By the thigh Mom located Zoe's hand. Never had touching a hand before given Lori such a thrill and with that thrill came hope. Hope that the two of them and their beloved dog could get out of this room and survive the wicked storm. Lori tried to shake Zoe, but she laid there limp as a doll.

Is Zoe okay? Could she be…?

Shaking off this negative thought Lori and Rosie strained harder, the dog's neck muscles bulging and tightening. There was a difference in the weight, Lori realized the dog must be grabbing a part of Zoe and tugging her. But to where? Lori felt Zoe's body sliding along the carpeted floor. Is Rosie so strong the canine could pull her and Zoe to safety?

The pressure in the room somehow changed, Lori could feel and tell that the way wind is whipping by her. What had happened?

"Are you with me Zoe?"

The lack of response disturbed Lori. That was bad news. Then Zoe started moving rapidly now, all Lori could do is keep a hold of Zoe's hand. They were propelled or dragged along the floor and out of the room. The door of the room slammed shut. Lori opened her eyes and found herself lying in the hotel hall gasping for air. Confused she sat up seeing two blurred figures and wiped her eyes. There standing beside her, and the fallen Zoe were two el Bomberos.

They were Mexican fireman in full outfits, a third Bombero crouched down on one knee and had a respirator over Zoe's mouth and nose.

Rosie stood close by Zoe, her tongue sticking out panting. Thank God they were saved and with that peaceful reassuring thought Lori passed out.

CHAPTER 8

DAY 3

Does the fun ever end for the Lund's? On the first day Rosie gets stuck in quicksand. The second day Mom falls into a sinkhole and Zoe battles a poisonous snake. Then that night a terrific tropical storm, what can happen today?

Returning to their hotel room or what is left of it, Mom and Zoe found that even the status of hallway was a disaster. Perhaps a few items could be saved, a toothbrush or even an article of clothes. They stood outside the door almost afraid to open it after last night's ordeal. Zoe leaned against the wall near the door.

"Do we have to go in Mom, it might be creepy in there." Zoe made a face. "Mom, I hear something in there."

"Your hearing things Zoe. Nothing is in there."

"There… Mom, I heard it again. Listen.'

With Lori tilted her head straining, trying to listen. Her ears perked up. "I did hear something."

Without a thought, Zoe used the keycard and opened the door. Rosie bounced past her into the room on guard duty. Stopping in the middle of the room, Rosie turning her head with her nose sniffing. A small bark sounded from under a messing bed, the other bed has been destroyed, tossed against the wall from the strong storm winds. Sticking her nozzle under the bed Rosie whimpered. Zoe went over and looked under the bed.

She said, "Awwh."

"What is going on Zoe? What's under the bed?"

"It's' so cute."

"What is so cute? What's going on?"

Reaching underneath the bread Zoe pulled out…a puppy. "It's so cute Mom, can we keep it?"

Barking, Rosie nuzzled the puppy.

"How did a puppy get in here?" Mom asked out loud not expecting an answer.

"That's easy Mom. It got lost in the storm and crawled in our broken window seeking shelter."

Mom smiled at her daughter's intelligence and reasoning. "You make it sound easy Zoe."

"Can we keep it Rosie needs a buddy."

"Slow down Zoe, it has to have an owner, puppy don't grow on trees."

"But trees do have *bark*." Zoe giggled at her own joke. "What kind of dog is it."

"Hand it to me Zoe."

"Mom I want to hold it for a while."

"Zoe c'mon!"

"Okay…Mom."

Reluctantly, Zoe handed over the dog. After all, her Mom is a veterinarian. Lori picked up the dog and examined it. The puppy managed to sneak a few licks of her tongue on Lori's hands and cheeks.

Mom held it up in the air, "It's a Golden Retriever and it's a boy."

As if on cue the puppy in its excitement, the young pup peed. The drops fell on the weather stained carpet. Mom shook her head, "For once Zoe I don't care if a dog pee's on carpet."

"That's for sure. What are we going to do with it— besides keep it." Zoe said smugly.

"I love you Zoe, but we should find the owner."

Pouting, Zoe looked sadly down, "If we must." Then she looked up and smiled. "What if we don't find the owner, then can we keep him."

"Don't you ever stop. We will keep him today, there is a lot of storm damage in the area. We need to clean him up, feed and give him water. Look at how wet and smelly his fur got"

Mom set the pup down on the floor, it yipped and then scampered over to Rosie lying on the floor. The puppy stopped at Rosie looked at the collie six times its size. The puppy yipped and pounced playfully on the large canine. Rosie barked, the bark sounded so loud that the pup ran back to Zoe and hid behind her legs. Mom and Zoe had to laugh at the sight.

"It might take a minute for the puppy to get used to Rosie." Explained Mom.

"Or the other way around, Rosie has to get used to a frisky playful little puppy."

"You go that right."

Picking up the puppy it licked Zoe's face, not that she minded. Zoe hugged it so hard the puppy seemed to squeak.

Be careful Zoe you don't want to break the puppy in two."

"Okay Mom, but he's so adorable." Zoe put the small dog down, it ran around a lap in the room and went back nestled between Zoe's legs.

Getting up, Rosie went to Zoe and poked her head between Zoe's legs to get to the puppy. The puppy whined whether in excitement or fear, Zoe did not know for sure.

Speaking up, Mom said. "Regardless of the puppy we need to see what we can save from this room, or we have no clothes to wear."

Zoe brightened up, "That means we need go shopping!"

"Say, that is a good idea!" Mom clapped her hands in excitement. "I can use that excuse with your father, but we still need to see what we can save. Let's start with the closet."

"And I will look in the drawers." Zoe added, she went and opened a drawer. "Owoo! Eck. This drawer is a mess, look at the water in it." Zoe pulled out a mangled shirt and pair of pants that dripped water. She threw them to the floor.

Rosie and the puppy ran over and started playing tug-of-war with a soaked pair of pants. Zoe started to stop them.

Mom watched them, "Let them play and tear them up."

"Really?"

"Sure, why not, they are already ruined."

"Okay guys get to it."

It's hard to believe how relaxed Mom is on vacation. If only she would be that way at home. Zoe grabbed a wet sock and tried to play tug of war with the puppy. The puppy took a nip and ran away, but Rosie joined in the fun and gave the sock a mighty tug. Shaking her head back and forth, Rosie yanked the sock out of Zoe's hand.

"Wow Mom! Sometimes I forgot how strong Rosie is."

Amazed, Lori watched the two dogs who were playing with a sock, it seemed that Rosie toyed about with the little guy. "Enough play let's get back to work and get organized, so we know what to buy when we go shopping. Make a pile of throwaways and a pile of keepers. Start now."

Just for fun Mom threw a wet shirt that hit Zoe in the stomach.

"Oh, you want to play Mom.—do you." Zoe picked up some clothes and threw them at Mom. For once she could get away with it.

A clothes fight broke out relieving the tension that Lori and Zoe had. It had been rough with all the damage to the room, their clothes and items destroyed by the wicked storm. The two dogs picked up the fallen items and played with them as well. The puppy found a sandal, snuck it to a corner of the room and contently chewed away on it. Rosie stuck her nose in a drawer that Zoe was working on. Zoe tossed a bunch of clothes in disgust onto the water-stained carpet.

Going through the next two drawers, Zoe managed to salvage a few items, which she put in a recycle plastic bag. She paused, wiped sweat from her face and gulped some water. The heat and humidity was blowing in through the broken windows. The room's air conditioning had been fried from the tropical monsoon.

"How we doing over there?" quizzed Mom.

"This is tough work, can't we throw everything away? It's all ruined anyway."

"Let's do our best to save what we can. I won't make it a big deal, we can quite in a half hour or so okay?"

Smartly, Mom gave Zoe a bite size chunk of a chore, not enough to overwhelm her young daughter.

"Okay...Mom. I want to over this before I get bored."

"Remember when we done, we will go shopping."

The distant sound of thunder came from outside the broken window. Is another storm rolling in?

"Hey Mom, what are we going to call the new puppy?"

"It's not our puppy, we will find the true owner or owner's."

Cleverly Zoe pointed at the dog, "It has no collar. What if we can't find the owner? Till then we need a name to call the little guy."

"We have to name him?"

As if on cue another bolt of thunder cracked outside, the sweet smell of ozone filled the room.

"That's it Mom, I got the name."

Giving in Mom asked, "So what it the little buggers name?"

"It's simple Mom he came in from a storm, and he's a survivor from a storm. Let's call him Thunder."

Thinking for a long moment, Loir agreed. "Not bad…not bad at all. In fact, its growing on me. Okay Thunder it is."

"Yea!"

"But only till we find him his real home."

Zoe's smile turned upside down into a frown. "Okay Mom."

Once again a thunderclap sounded, little Thunder raced across the room and nested between Zoe's legs, she bent over and patted the dog.

Checking her smartphone, "Time to quit." Mom picked up two of the recycle bags. "Grab two bags and let's go.

"Okay Mom." Zoe bent over and grabbed a pair of bags.

Mom headed to the door and motioned to go.

"I do want to go to our new room." In a higher loud voice, "Come Rosie and Thunder. Let's go for a walk?!?"

Being dogs they jumped up to their feet and followed them to the door and down the hall to their new room. The dogs were ushered into the new motel room and given water. The two soiled bags were deposited in the bathtub, the other two by the closet. Lori and Zoe paused for a moment calming themselves. Rosie stayed in the main room and Zoe put Thunder, in the bathroom since they didn't want the whole hotel suite messed up by a puppy.

They gave each other a sly smile.

The saying all women like to say, Mom and daughter looked at each other and smile and said," LETS GO SHOPPING!"

CHAPTER 9

Everything you need to buy is at Galeri'as Altama. One of Mexico's finest malls, the stores range from Aldolfo Dominguez or American Eagle, to the savory tasty burgers La Ruta del Sabor, the Tommy Hilfiger stylish fashion line and you could dance your way through Zumba.

But today Lori and Zoe were not dancing, they were shopping! While they carried their bags of goodies, they had mental baggage on their mind. The two Lund women carried a large range of feelings and thoughts. Depressed and battled by the events of the accidents and the tropical storm, yet somehow they were happy to be alive and hoping to see their family later today. Lori sure could use a hug from her family. The finding of the puppy did help punctuated their happiness and elated their mood.

Walking up the mall ramp, the mother and daughter took in the bright and beautiful multilevel mall curling around a large open concept design. The center or *el centro* of the atrium resembled a small tropical jungle. Native shoppers were sitting in overstuffed white bean bags that surrounded the floral area, Slowing to a stop, Zoe pointed. Mom followed Zoe's gaze. Perched on a stand in the middle of the mall floor sprawled an enormous blue crab!

It looked to be the King Crab of the mall, if not the world, unless you saw a monster horror movie. It stood about 5 meters tall and just as wide, with colorful seashells plastered on its giant shell back.

Wow! Zoe knew that after the enormous blue crab she had seen everything.

She would latter find out that would never be true.

An hour quickly went by, Mexican pesos were traded for clothes and other items. Lori would converse in Spanish, which Zoe occasionally understood the main words. Like, *Que tal*-what's up, *Listo*- ready and *claro qui si*--of course. Lori always said *Gracias* at the end. Which means, thank you.

Lunch went by fast, they had two raspberry lemonade, two orders of avocado chicken enchiladas and a shared a delicious crunchy cheese crisp. As soon as they finished the meal both ladies wanted to get going. They had to dash back to the new room, unpack and prepare to get to the airport for the 5 o'clock arrival of Steven, Zac and Uncle Scott. Of course, there were the dogs to be taken care of.

A waitress appeared, took the bill and Mom's credit card. She scanned the card, Lori signed and left a substantial *Propina*—the tip. As Lori finished signing, she started to slide the credit card into the bag, her smartphone rang. Lori fumbled trying to put the credit card away and get the phone out of her side bag at the same time.

"Olla!" Lori answered seeing the image of Steven.

"Mi cara mia. My dear. Que tal?"

"I'm fine Steven what's going on?" Knowing the Steven often laid it on sweet when something bad happened.

"The three of us are stuck at the Chicago O'Hara Airport. The plane developed a mechanical problem. We won't make it down there till morning tomorrow, and that's taking the *red eye* flight."

Oh, I am sorry to hear that honey. Is Zac okay? How is he handling this?"

"He's just fine, Zac gets to see some distant cousins. We are going to stay at the Stihl's house."

"You mean Carl and Adele Sthil. Last I remember they were living in Elk Grove?"

"Yes," Steven replied. "I already called and checked. They have that old fashion open door policy and I using my cousin calling card."

That's great I haven't seen them in forever. But it still sucks that I don't get to see my husband tonight."

Steven's tone softened and deepened. "Me too honey, me too."

Seeing the look upon her mother's face of hurt and sorrow. "Mom?"

231

Noticing her daughter , Mom forced a smile. "It's okay Zoe. Dad…Zoe says hi and hello to Zac."

"Well Dad says, Zac and him say hi back."

Attempting a smile, Zoe took her last sip of tea, and she made a loud slurping sound. Mom frowned briefly. Lori and Steven talked for a long moment or a brief one depending on how you count a moment.

Finally, "I will text you the Airline, Flight times and Flight numbers and where you two can pick us up."

"We only have a RAV 4 Steven, that's too small for five us, plus the luggage and two dogs."

"Two dogs!" Steven exclaimed. "How did you get two dogs…let me guess. Zoe is up to something. Right?"

"You do know our daughter, apparently we have a new dog."

"Just what we need, another dog." Steven's voice sounded strained.

"At least for the moment. It's a stray Golden Retriever puppy we rescued from the terrible storm last night. It's only 4 to 5 months old."

Quickly, Lori explained the story and Steven knowing he couldn't do anything about it had to go along.

"But wait a minute Lori, enough with the puppy. How will we all get away from the airport?"

"That's easy enough. I will charter the hotel bus to pick us all up. It will be quite a handful, with Rosie and the new puppy, Thunder aboard."

You could hear Steven echo the word "Thunder" as Lori quickly said "Bye.' She tapped the smartphone and stowed it away in her side bag.

"Let's get going Zoe we have one last stop on the way home. We need to get a collar, lease and some puppy supplies."

Instantly Zoe stood up, "Okay Mom you don't have to say that twice, I'm already fond of the little guy. So don't forget the puppy treats that we will need for training him and of course the training pads for puppy pee."

Both females giggled at that thought.

After a short drive they pulled in the parking lot of a pet food and supply chain called Petco Tampico. Lori wondered what geniuses had thought up that name, but they do have a great Google rating. The location also seemed safe and convenient on the way back to the Capybara Hotel. One has to be careful driving anywhere in Mexico with the high crime rate, and the Cartels and their "tell, tell" signs. It did not always make it comfortable driving in certain areas.

Scanning the area, Lori had picked a safe parking spot, as safe as possible in today's wicked world. She parked the Toyota and climbed out keeping up her guard as Zoe got out. A wave of heat greeted them as they crossed the hot asphalt. Entering the store there were no perfume smell like many department stores, but rather a store scent to cover up the animal odors. The ladies wandered around taking in the sights for a few moments and then got down to business. Surprisingly they talked only a little, the shopping went quickly, partially because both of them were getting worn out and wanted to get back to the room and check on the canines. The other part that went well is they agreed on a collar for Thunder in the first ten minutes.

They went to the checkout counter. Speaking in Spanish Mom paid the cashier. Supplies were bought. bags were stuffed and loaded. Off went Mom and Zoe in the RAV 4 back to the Hotel room. Zoe tapped her finger on the armrest the whole way back extremely anxious to see the new puppy.

Standing outside the Hotel room door, Zoe pressed her ear against the door trying to listen.

"I don't hear anything Mom, is that a good thing?"

"Perhaps Zoe, let's open the door and find out."

Swiping the keycard, Zoe opened the door. Rosie barked within a second of the door opening, staring at the doorway half growling, the hair in her main ruffled. A wave of recognition overcame her, and she trotted over to be petted. Scratching sounded on the bathroom door, followed by whimpering. Zoe took off for the door, opened it and Thunder leaped at her. Raising the little guy, Zoe suffered being licked by him. Well, she didn't' suffer much, in fact she enjoyed it until…

The sharp tone of Mom's voice sounded like a whip. "Zoe! Put that dog down right now. We don't' want to teach him bad manners by licking people. In fact, we should put in some obedience training today, particularly with the potty part."

Of course, Mom was right, a dog must be trained young. Zoe remembered what her mother had said that a dog is only as good as its owner.

"Okay Mom, let's get out the doggie treats and start."

"Nice try young lady, we need to unpack and get the whole room organized first. Remember the men will be here tomorrow."

"I'm on it."

That motivated Zoe to quickly unpack everything, so she could train and play with the puppy later, and of course with Rosie. At Petco they had bought a tug-of -war toy she couldn't wait to try out.

"I'm on it Mom, perhaps we should take the dogs our for a quick walk first."

"That's a great idea! They have been here awhile."

At first Thunder fought about having his new collar put on, then finally after some coaching he calmed down. Mom and Zoe took a quick walk outside with the two dogs.

Outside in the parking lot Mom smiling mischievously and playfully, Mom said, "You take Thunder, and I will take Rosie."

At first it seemed like a good idea to Zoe. Then she realized what her mother had done. The puppy tugged and yanked like he had never been walked before. It seemed like Zoe was herding cats. After the difficult walk Zoe had learned a lesson or two about puppy's. Getting back to the Hotel room, seemed more like a relief to Zoe. Which surprised her.

"Mom has this dog been trained at all?"

"It doesn't seem like it. Maybe the storm upset it, and the loss of its owner now has Thunder confused. Dogs need structure and a routine."

Pouting, Zoe made a sad face.

"Don't worry honey, we will get him going till we fine the owner." Mom started unpacking.

Zoe's frown turned into a smile. "I know he will be okay."

"Why, Zoe?"

"Because you're the best veterinarian in the world."

Putting away a shirt, taking in the statement, Mom paused. She simply said, "Thanks Zoe, but we're in this together."

The next hour of packing went by. Then the Lund's and the two dogs went outside. They started with the basics, like how to sit. Which went by example, Rosie would sit, and lay down, Thunder learned how to follow. The puppy almost got as far how to shake and that was about it.

"Mom, I wanted to teach Thunder how to shake and fist bump. Zoe seemed a bit bummed out.

"It's only been an hour of training, he will get better. We've trained Rosie for a couple of years. They say patience is a virtue"

"So, they say." mumbled Zoe. Like any young person she expects results now.

"Then keep at it Zoe, you'll do fine."

Zoe worked with Thunder for another ten minutes until Mom said no more. Returning to the new room they got to it, knowing they had to finish up because the time was important. The next hour sped by, a combination of unpacking, arranging and organizing. The dogs were completely worn out. Rosie lay in the corner of the room, with the sleeping puppy. Half asleep, and half-awake, the collie watching the three

237

of them at work. Finally, Rosie gave up and drifted to sleep.

"Looks like we're about done and organized. Thank you young lady you have been quite the helper."

"No problem Mom, I'm highly motivated."

"Motivated by what?" Asked Mom closing a drawer.

"By swimming at the pool."

"That's right in all the craziness we've had only one short swim. I'm so sorry I know how much you like to swim. Let's find a way to get out of here and get our feet wet."

"I want to get my whole body wet Mom, and I have a new two piece swimsuit to try out."

"Well so do I." Said Lori holding up a leopard print one piece suit, that highlighted her strawberry blonde hair. "I hope you father likes it."

Checking out her mother's trim athletic body. "I'm sure Dad will Mom."

Zoe was old enough to agree with her mother.

CHAPTER 10

The pool water surprised Zoe as she dove into it, being much colder than she thought it would be. Zoe's head popped up out of the chlorinated water her strawberry curls plastered to her head.

"Mom, it's cold."

"Probably from the storm last night." Called back Lori standing at the edge of the pool drinking peach iced tea. "In that case I will use the stairs and get in slowly.

Moving around in the water, "Once you get in you get used to it." Zoe admitted. "But it's kinda cool."

The Hotel Capybara had a magnificent pool that was kidney shaped and over two hundred meters long, in the middle stood a cement island with a "kiddie" pool. Two arched bridges crossed over the pool that lead to "kiddie island."

The pool's bridge and the fountains light up spectacularly at night for the enjoyment of both children and adults. During the day, multiple fountains of water were spraying everywhere, in direction and different heights, to keep the toddles and their parents cooled off from the harsh heat of the tropical sun.

Swimming in a backward lope underwater, Zoe enjoyed being underwater as much as on the surface. Coming up for a beath of air, she broke the surface water beading on her eye goggles.

"Are you ever getting in Mom?"

"Absolutely Zoe after the day we had, I'm almost done with my tea." Mom took a final sip leaving only the melting ice and sat down the plastic glass. "On second thought, I might as well get in all at once."

Walking over to the diving board and in three quick steps Lori sprung off board into a jackknife, hitting the water cleanly. Her feet hardly making a splash. Zoe thought it was great how both of her parents kept so trim and fit.

Mom's head pop up, "Your right the water is cold, Dad always says cold water is *invigorating."*

"Swimming some laps will warm us up."

"You don't have to tell me twice, let's get going." Mom agreed. She took off and Zoe followed.

The two ladies swam a few laps, which is quite a feat in the ginormous long pool. Occasionally they slowed and circled about a few ignorant people in the pool that got in their way. They finished the laps then played and mucked about as content as a pair of dolphins for a while.

Swimming over to the edge of the pool, "I'm hungry Mom." Said Zoe half expecting to be told to wait for dinner.

"No problem, let's order a snack to hold us over." Mom flagged a waiter down. "Order anything you want."

"Okay," Zoe said cautiously wondering if Mom would change her mind.

Knowing her daughter, Mom said, "After the last few days eat whatever you want I'm just glad all of us are alive."

"That's the truth Mom, thank God we are all alive and now we got the little puppy."

That comment did not get a response. The waiter made his way over dodging a small kid on the loose. He presented them with a small, laminated pool side menu, consisting of appetizer's with a few sandwiches. On the flip side were several exotic drinks both alcoholic and non-alcoholic.

Eying the menu hungrily, Zoe looked at her mother. Lori nodded okay.

Promptly Zoe ordered, "One bag of potato chips, an order of nachos, a ham and cheese sandwich." She hesitated and quicky added in, "And for good measure a fudge drumstick."

Without a blink Mom ordered two ice waters with lemon, and some Tortilla Roll ups that are called "Pinwheels" in Mexico.

They next hour they ate, swam some more and worked on their tan. For once thing's they had a calm and relaxing afternoon.

Later that day:

Tossing down her menu on the restaurant table, Zoe said. "There are so many things to choose from Mom, there must be a million types of pasta on this menu. I thought we were in Mexico, not Italy. Why are there so many Italian ristorante's here?"

"Great question Zoe. I believe that's because there are so many tourists. Think about it? Pizza is the second favorite food after the Mexican food."

As the waitress poured more water in their glasses. Mom paused for the moment. The waitress left.

"I get it Mom. Pizza and pasta is inexpensive to make."

"That's right, it makes a good profit for the restaurant. Also, there are a lot of Italian's that live in Mexico too." Mom paused looking at the menu. "Let's get our order in."

The waitress came back, ready to take their orders. Zoe after all the time and consideration she spent

242

with the menu she ended up ordering shrimp and angel hair pasta her regular favorite.

Mom shook her head, *Why bother.*

Deciding, Mom ordered in Spanish, "The Ceasar salad and Chicken Marsala, in a mushroom sauce and creamy short-grain rice called Risotto for a side." She liked the deep nutty and slightly sweet flavor of the meal. The waitress placed on the table a platter of bread, butter, parmesan cheese and garlic spread on the table and left.

"Swimming sure works up an appetite Mom."

 "And don't forget the shopping also."

"Mom?" Zoe picked up a piece of bread and buttered it, then shook on some parmesan.

"Yes, dear."

"I already miss the new puppy."

'I'm sure Rosie will take good care of him." Mom added garlic spread to her bread.

Holding the bread in front her mouth before she took a bite, Zoe aksed, "But who will take care of Rosie?"

"Rosie is a full grown collie, nothing is going to happen to her. She can take care of herself." To emphasize the comment Lori took a bit of the delicious warm bread.

"I...I know Mom. It's not the dog I'm worried about.

"What is it honey, you can tell me."

"But." Zoe wiped her mouth with a napkin. "I hate to say it, I'm home sick... at least a little."

Understanding all the trauma that they had gone through the last couple of days. Mom said, "That's only natural, Steven, Zac and Uncle Scott will be here tomorrow. That will cheer you up."

Chewing on her bread and now enjoying it, Zoe said, "Mom, don't say anything, but I will even be glad to see Zac."

Mom paused on her bite, but only for a second. "I'm sure he will be glad to see you too."

"Yeah right."

"At least Dad and Uncle Scott will be glad to see you."

"That's right Uncle Scott is coming with."

"That's great Mom. I miss Uncle Scott."

Zoe couldn't deny that it had been a while since she had seen Uncle Scott, and she missed him. Somehow he was a blast to play with for a tough guy. They talked about home for a few minutes until the food showed up. It looked appetizing and smelled wonderful.

The waitress gave a slight bow saying, "Una Provecho!" and left.

We all know how restaurants work, things do go wrong at times. Mom took her first   bite of her Chicken Marsala. A large piece of mushroom fell landing in the table. Resisting a giggle, Zoe knew how much her brother Zac would have laughed and made a big deal about it. Mom swiped it up with a napkin making it disappear.

Sometimes we all wish things would disappear so easily.

CHAPTER 11

Day 4

"Don't do it. Don't throw me into the pool." Standing by the pool in a bright floral two piece swimsuit, Zoe danced about teasing Uncle Scott at the edge of the pool.

Making a pretend lunge at her, Scott missed. Zoe giggled, easily escaped and moved over to the edge of the pool. She presented herself as a moving target.

"I'll get you yet young lady." Scott said in a gruff voice. "You won't escape my clutches. This time.

That only made Zoe giggle louder.

Brother Zac butted in, "I can help, let me get her."

Scott stuck out his bronzed arm. "No, you can't, this is between Zoe and me." Declared Scott.

"You can't get me. You can't get me…"

Lunging at her, Uncle Scott went about half his speed. Zoe darted about and executed a hip throw that sent Scott sailing into the pool. Which sent him flying, a mass of tan muscles and limbs. Spreading out his thick arms Scott hit the water with a mighty splash. He came up and exaggerated sputtering water out of his mouth.

"You will regret this when I get my hands on you." Scott retorted. "I'll never live it down being throw into a pool—by a girl."

Laughing so hard that Zoe about fell over, the rest of the family joined in on the fun. As Scott started to get out of the pool, Zoe immediately scampered behind father, Steven.

Trying not to laugh, Steven said, "You can't hide behind me girl, you have to fight your own battles. Even if they are with *a border agent*."

Resolving the matter, Zoe ran toward the pool and leaped over Scott as he was getting out. Swinging his mighty arms at Zoe, Scott missed her on purpose. Diving into the pool, the young girl swam away underwater like she was being chased by a shark. Standing up, Scott watched Zoe propel away. Suddenly a pair of hands pushed Scott back into the pool.

SPLASH!

Receiving his second dip in the pool today, Scott's sandy colored head popped up to see Zac laughing bent over and pointing a finger at him.

"Ha, ha, ha…ha. I got you Uncle Scott. I got you good."

247

"Oomph!"

Splash!

Zac had been shoved into the pool—by Steven. The youth went with the flow and continued toward the bottom of the deep end and safety swam out a distance to be in the clear. Or so he thought till a hand yanked sharply on his ankle. Scott had swam underwater following the rascal and caught Zac. Both Scott and Zac surfaced chuckling, playing, splashing and thrashing about. An elderly lady slowly swimming laps stopped, glared at them and said something not so nice in Spanish. Ignoring her complaints and bad words, Scott started swimming away. Promptly Zac followed, not wanting to get into any more trouble.

Shaking her head, Lori smiled at the sight of all the entertainment her family had been providing her with. She opened her pool bag, took out a Nora Roberts romance novel and lay down on a lounge chair to read and relax.

Going over Steven kissed his wife's forehead. "Nothing like a relaxing vacation right dear?"

"Wait till I tell you about our 'relaxing vacation' Steven."

"Oh?" Steven's auburn eyes got big knowing his wife.

"Tell you what, apply sunscreen on me and I just might share a few details."

She reached in a got out a bottle of SPF 30 spray and one of SPF 15 bronzing lotion. Lori went on talking about the quicksand and the Cenote sinkhole. For the moment she left out the parts about the vine snake and the rope snapping. Also, Lori would save the surprise about the storm and the puppy for later. The look on the Lund men's faces would be delightful when they saw the puppy back at the hotel room.

All in all, an average couple of days for the life of the Lund family. Meanwhile, Zoe, Zac and Uncle Scott where having a blast in the pool.

"Thow me the basketball Uncle." Zac begged. "C'mon throw it."

"No throw it to me." Cried out Zoe looking cute as could, and she did a good job of it.

Scott said, "I don't know. I can't play favorites…can I?"

He faked whipping it at Zoe and blasted it at Zac. It hopped across the water like skipping a stone. Zac's right hand snatched it off a bounce and tossed it to Zoe. Caught off guard by the move the ball hit her squarely on the nose. She winced for a moment but had to play it tough. Picked up the floating ball, Zoe held it as the Senor female swimmer came by doing breaststrokes.

She paused and mumbled, "Ninos, es muy local."

Zoe understood but ignored her, which made the lady more irritated.

Holding her sore nose, she used the excuse, "The sun was in my eyes Zac, or I would have caught it."

"Yea, yea Sis. It's no big deal, you're not bleeding?"

"Uncle Scott!?!"

"Just throw the ball Zoe and I will get us all ice cream later at the snack bar. Let's go over to the basketball hoop and make some shots."

That way nobody get mad or hurt. Scott hoped.

Some kids were just finishing playing at the basketball stand at the edge of the pool and left a floating ball. Great, now the Lund's had two basketball to play around with. Double the pleasure double the fun! Or perhaps as the Lund's are used to; double the trouble.

Making a shot into the basket, Zac said, "Nothing but net."

Zoe's shot rolled around the rim and went in. Raising his left hand, Scott nodded. Zac tossed a basketball out to Scott. His bronze hand arched into the air, making a hook shot. It also went in, three for three is always a good start.

Holding hands, Lori felt better, "I am so glad you're here Steven. It's been rough for me and Zoe the last couple of days."

Steven stopped applying the sunscreen and moved his hand to his wife's shoulder. "I'm sorry to hear that Lori. Getting down here has been no picnic either. The plane had a mechanical problem, but it's good they detected it. If you know what I mean."

"Hey at least you got to see family, how are the Stihl's?"

"Doing good. They had no major bad news to share. You know what they say, no news is good news."

"People do say that."

"Yes they do but were all alive, that's the important part.

Lori rolled over on her back and took the bottle from Steven and started applying sunscreen on her legs. "I thought Zoe and I would spend lots of time every day at the pool, and this is the first time I actually get to relax here."

Checking out at the pool, Steven noticed its inviting water. "We are both here as a family. Every day is a new day, and I have to say a swim does sound good."

"Let's order some Iced tea and talk for a few more minutes, Then we can go swimming."

Inside Steven groaned, He wanted to get wet in this intense heat. But knowing that Lori liked her tea, and she definitely liked to talk.

"Sure honey, I'm might thirsty and would like a tea and talk."

"You're such a good husband and I have a lot to say."

Steven sat down on the lounge besides her to listen to his wife. A tough job for any husband, but soon a waiter came over to take their order, interrupting the conversation. The waiter left and Lori started right away talking up a storm. While listening, Steven started watching Zoe and Scott tossing the basketball about.

CHAPTER 12

Yelling, "I got it." Scott lifted the ball to shoot…

Suddenly Zac slapped it out of Scott's hands.

"Hey now!" Yelled Scott.

Zac jumped to shoot, and Scott got a hand on it partially blocking the attempt. The ball went wild as things sometimes go. The ball landed right on the head of the senor lady's as she swam by and bounced off.

"Oww!" The elder lady yelled. She paused, stood up and rubbed the top of her head. She lifted her goggles and glared at Zac and Scott.

Now a series of mistakes would happen.

The lady used profanity in Spanish, which Scott understanding Spanish made him mad. He knew his nephew and niece might understand some of it. The lady, *not so ladylike* continued to cuss up a storm of bad and vulgar words. Her hands gesturing as she spoke. Scott grabbed a hand, which was probably another mistake, and told her.

"Callarse la boca!"

Her face redden more and not from the sun and as she yanked her had away, Scott quickly let go.

"I will report this to the Pool manager young man. You will be sorry you touched me." In fury with her goggles on her forehead, she half-walked half-swam away.

Shrugging his broad shoulders, Scott wondered what could he do?

An expression of alarm crossed Zac's face. "Sorry about that Uncle. We were just playing around."

"No big deal Zac, the damage is already done."

"I didn't mean to hit her."

"I know that, just forget it and be more careful in the future.

Wading over, Zoe stated, "You guys sure can get into trouble." She snickered knowing she had also help irritate the older woman.

"We don't need help getting in trouble. We do a good job at it ourselves." Zac added.

The three of them laughed. It did seem sort of funny at the time. Scott settled the matter and picked up a basketball and tossed it to Zoe. She eyed the backboard and shot the ball, it bounced off the rim. Zac scurried in for the rebound and slammed it home. Soon Scott forgetting the woman found himself smiling again, playing with Zac and Zoe. He looked over at Steven and Lori. They were drinking tea in fancy cups and holding hands.

"It's so hot that I am Kentucky fried." Steven declared trying to be funny. "But Lori enough, I need a dip in the pool. Would you like to join me?" Steven stood up, all 6' 2" or 1.85 meters of himself.

"Yes dear, the sun does bake you down here, that's for sure. A swim does sound good. Then I need to shower and do my hair tonight anyway." Lori got up and stretched in her leopard print a one piece swimsuit. She pulled her strawberry blonde hair back into a tie. "Shall we cool off?"

Steven did not have to be told twice. They went to the pool Lori walked into the shallow end. Steven went to the deep in and dove in. The Lifeguard ignored the dive. The couple met in the middle of the elongated pool.

"Hey Dad!" Zoe wadded over and splashed him.

Steven half splashed back. "Let's get Mom."

"Okay." Zoe agreed and started splashing Lori.

Who did not like it one bit.

"Okay, okay guys, for getting me wet." Mom said sarcastically. "Later." Mom dove underwater and propelled away.

255

Wading over Scott said, "About time you got in bro. It's stinking hot down here in Mexico."

"Don't I know it, but Lorelie and I had some catching up to do."

Understanding, Scott nodded. "That means she talked your ear off—right."

"Something like that." Steven mumbled.

Zac's head popped up from the surface of the pool. He had just swum over underwater. "Hey Dad want to swim a couple of laps."

"That sounds good son. Let's go."

Crying out, "Okay Dad. Let's race, go!" Off went the two Lund men.

A deep Hispanic voice called out. "Hey rubio! (blondie) You there. I need to talk to you."
Scott pointed to himself. "Me?"

"Si, you. Come here now." A tall dark haired man in slacks and a polo with the emblem of the Hotel Capybara stood there

"What does he want Uncle Scott?" Asked Zoe.

"Let's go and find out."

Scott headed to the edge of the pool with Zoe in tow. The large man had his hands on his hips.

"Que pasa?"

"Get out of the pool senor we need to talk."

Puzzled Scott and Zoe climbed up the ladder and stood beside the man, who towered over Scott who stood about 1.8 meters.

"What is going on?" Scott inquired with a dripping wet Zoe standing beside him.

The elder woman who had been hit by the ball appeared by the side of the man, wearing a swim cover of pink flamingos all over it. A swim cover so bright you almost needed sunglasses to look at it.

"This is the man. He is the man that grabbed my wrist and hurt me." She held her right wrist like it hurt unbearably.

The man frowned. "I am Jose, the manager. You will apologize to my Aunt Maria right now and we will think about not calling the police and having you arrested for harming her."

Her nephew is the Hotel manager? Scott shook his head.

Can the Lund's ever have a normal day?

Scott drew himself to his full height, yet still a few centimeters short of Jose. "I will apologize if she apologizes for using profanity in front of children."

"I did no such thing." The woman claimed.

"She cusses better than a pirate." stated Scott.

With a sharp intake of breath, the woman insisted. "I do not! You are rude."

Speaking up, Zoe said, "She is mean and says lots of bad words that I am not allowed to repeat."

Puzzled, Jose turned to his Aunt Maria. "Is this true? You cussed in front of children which are guests of the Hotel."

Stamping her right foot on the cement. "Never Jose. I speak the truth."

Tilted his head sideways, Jose looked at Scott. "You are in trouble mister…?"

"Lund, Scott Lund."

"Perhaps Senor Lund, we should let the police clear up this matter, no?" Jose leaned closer to Scott.

"Why don't we both apologize and forget the whole thing?" Aske Scott.

A blank look crossed Jose's face.

Fidgeting around, her fists clenching, an idea sprang to Zoe's mind. She took a step and accidentally slipped on purpose. Zoe bumped into Maria's hip.

Maria exploded in anger. "Why you little dirty rotten little b**** and further more….Blah, blah, blah." (More bad words)

Jose shrunk several centimeters hearing the bad words springing out of his Aunt's mouth.

Frowning Jose said, "I must apologize Senor for my Aunt. Please forgive me. I also apologize to you young lady. I almost made a mistake. Can I offer the two of you complementary food or drinks?"

Zoe started to say, "Yes…"

Scott cut her off. "It is not necessary. We are fine. You can have the difficulty of dealing with your Aunt."

The Aunt looked like she wanted to crawl under a rock and hide.

"Come with me Aunt Maria, we need to go have a serious talk."

"But they started it…"

Maria frowned so big a bird could have perched on her lower lip.

Jose took by her arm, and they left. Zoe and Scott fist bumped each other, trying not to laugh.

It ended up being a great day at the pool in spite of things. At least nobody got arrested. The Lund's left the pool, went to their rooms to get cleaned up before dinner. Walking back to the hotel rooms, the family stopped at their door.

Scott paused, "See you guys in a bit." He waved goodbye and took off for his room. The Lund's all waved back.

Holding a towel and bag, Zoe asked, "Father, you can open the Hotel door my hands are full."

""Sure, just give me a moment."

For some reason unknown to Dad, Zoe tried hard not to giggle or laugh. Steven took the key card out of Mom's bag and swiped it. Steven opened the door, both him and Zac entered. Springing to her feet, Rosie barked twice and wagged her tale at Zac.

"Here Rosie." Zac called out and Rosie trotted over to him. A smaller barking sounded, actually more of a yipping. Thunder raced over to Zoe and Zoe petted the little guy. Thunder went over and sniffed Zac, his tail wagging crazy like.

"Two dogs!?!" Steven paused stunned by the sight. "Wait you did say something about two dogs. Lori—explain!"

Laughed out loud with her mother, they both said, "Surprise!"

Zoe pointed at Zac's feet. "I guess the second surprise is on you Zac."

In his excitement, Thunder had peed on Zac's Croc's.

Zac called out loud, "ZOE!"

CHAPTER 13

Nothing like an evening on a beach watching a Caribbean sea sunset. A picture of beauty, a tranquil moment of peace and enjoyment. Sunset, where the golden-orange globe of the sun sinks into the emerald, blue sea. The rolling waves of the sea crashing against the sandy beach, like background music. Crisp winds blowing in the salty smell of ocean. The sun hovering over the horizon, a huge glowing disc so large because of the equator horizontal latitude.

Sitting with her family at the beachside restaurant, Zoe admired the sight, putting a mental picture in her head. The sun could never look like this in the Mid-West where the Lund's called home. Zoe looked at her mother and father holding hands gazing out at the sunset. Scott seemed deep in thought and Zac taking multiple pictures with his smartphone.

This is the vacation she wanted, time with family. A time out from the world. Zoe's mind drifted back to the dogs. How much she loved Rosie and what were they going to do with the new puppy? It had been actually fun, her and Zac taking the two dogs for a walk before supper. At first Zac clowned around as normal, then he calmed down and seemed to enjoy walking Thunder. Often Zac would smile at the puppy as it constantly ran, pulling on the lead, his curious nose smelling and sniffing everything he could. Rosie would lead the way, frequently stopping for Thunder, like a patient mother. It seemed she had taken a liking to the puppy as well. After the walk they returned to their room, got cleaned up and supper was becoming another pleasant memory as well. The waiters came over and started to clean the table, which broke the mood for the moment.

Standing up and stretching Steven asked, "Anybody want more desert?"

The table still laid littered with crumbs of cornflakes and cinnamon from the "Mexican" fried ice cream. The ice cream treat had been frozen hard and breaded, then quickly deep fried creating a warm crispy shell around the still-cold ice cream. No one answered, not even Zac who had just finished off his third helping and wiped his mouth.

Shrugging his broad shoulders at the lack of answers, Steven said, "Whatever?" and sat down.

"What's next everybody?" Asked Lori.

The discussion instantly started, a blur of the family's voices with many different suggestions and ideas, a movie, a walk, even another swim. The talk of Lori and Zoe's misadventures came up. Lori gave her version of Rosie, and the quicksand rescue that Zoe had helped in.

Tapping her glass with a spoon, Zoe announced, "Listen up everybody. I made up a joke about the quicksand."

Smiling, Mom knew what Zoe was going to say.

"Okay...let's hear it." Scott asked. "I can always use a good joke that I can tell at work. Us border agents are never stressed or tensed."

"C'mon daughter tell us the joke." Added Dad.

Beaming at the attention, Zoe cleared her throat. "Okay...What do you call four Mexicans caught in quicksand?"

A couple of smart aleck answers floated around the table.

Finally, Zoe raised her hands up and outward. "Quatro cinco!"

The entire table burst out with laughter. A waiter walking by, he paused and only heard the punch line. His eyes wrinkled together, *what?*

Repeating it, Scott told the joke in Spanish.

His face went blank for a moment, then a smile appeared on his mouth. "Si, muy bien, muy bien." He kept chuckling as he made his way back to the kitchen. There he would retell the joke, perhaps claiming he made it up.

Taking a sip of Iced tea, Lori started on the Cenote sinkhole story. She told the story of falling, getting knocked unconscious and her rescue by Zoe and Rosie with emotion and feeling. Especially the part about the vine snake battle with Rosie. Everybody listened intently, with the miracle that there were no interruptions. To cap off the story, Lori proudly looked at Zoe.

"That's my daughter. She saved the day, or I might not even be here right now."

Her cheeks blushed without make up. Zoe fidgeted about uncomfortably in her chair.

"Thank you Zoe." Mom tapped Zoe on the shoulder.

Surprising modest for a young person she changed the topic. Zoe mentioned, "Hey everybody? How about the Arcade at the Hotel Capybara?"

The table went silent, but only for a moment. Suddenly all at once the Lund's ideas bouncing everywhere.

Steven pounded his fist twice on the table apologetically to quiet everyone. "Listen up everybody the Arcade idea sounds great and fun. We could have a Lund family Battle Royal."

"That's right!" agreed Zoe. "I have been here for days and never got to play in the hotel game room."

Excitedly Zac said, "Sounds good to me Sis, cause I will kick your rear into gear."

Rising to the occasion. "Zac, I can beat you in Donkey Kong anytime."

"Us older folks can play just as well." Lori commented.

Lifted up his hand motioning, Steven said, "Let the games begin. Waiter bring the check!"

Bleeps, bloops, booms and the sounds of car engines revving greeted the Lund's as they entered the Game room. They were greeted by flashing neon lights and with the sound of an artificial crowd cheering for the gamers. Further sounds of crashing noises, explosions, squealing tires and the chiming bings made from pinball machines were heard. It looked like a couple dozen players, consisting of adults, youths and kids were occupied.

The party had already started.

Swiping his credit card for tokens, Steven disturbed them to everybody. Off the Lund's went, Scott and Steven to play air hockey. Lori, Zoe, and Zac went over to the games that were the oldies and the goodies. The Game room still had Donkey Kong and Pac-Man.

On the way across the Game room some young kids were playing a game much like Whack-A Mole. The funny part is that they were whacking avocados instead of mole's. In Mexico the game is called,

Guac-A-Mole. It gets even better, on the wall stood a video game called Guacamelee.

Excitedly pointing, Zoe squealed, "I've heard of that game." As they went closer, a young girl left the video game.

Holding out a token, Zac explained the game to his Mother, "*On the Day of the Dead*, a farmer Juan explores an open world, he explores and battles enemies. When he defeats them he collects coins and buys new skills. There can also be a second co-player."

"Count me in Zac and I will destroy you."

"We will see about that sis."

Letting the youth's start their battle, Lori looked over at her husband. Steven was battling with Scott in Air Hockey. Steven had just scored a goal. He jumped up and down in joy.

"Lucky shot Steven. That took quite a weird bounce."

"Maybe?" Steven dropped the puck and whipped it at Scott's goal.

Scott blocked it left handed and shot it back. Steven deflected it. The puck whipped across the table. Scott stabbed at it, the puck went flying off the table skittering across the floor.

"Not so rough bro." Steven cautioned.

"Nothing like brotherly rivalry." Going over and picking up the puck Scott returned to the table and suddenly dropped the puck. It shot it like a cannon and scored on his older brother."

Scott didn't have to say, *I told you so.*

"Clever brother." Steven frowned, picked it up and fired a puck back at Scott. Scott blocked it and knocked it back. The two brothers went at it and battled at a speed beyond normal men. The puck became a blur and the sounds of hitting the puck were like firecrackers going off. A full minute of chaos went by, and spectators gathered around the table watching the performance of the Lund brothers. The clank of the puck announced the scoring of another goal. So fast that no one had seen it go in. Scott gave out a hoot of victory and won the game 10 to 8. Steven had not even seen the shot.

He set down his paddle. "Great game Scott. I remember back when I used to beat you."

"Yeah like when I was ten or twelve." Scott said dryly.

"Well, I did beat you... then." Steven glanced over checking on his family.

Zac and Zoe were yelling at the game, he thought he heard them say something about zombies. The world seem full of make believe zombies. Why shouldn't Mexico had their own version as well. Scott went for water and Steven walked over and watched his "Power kids" fight it out.

As bad luck would have it, both Zoe and Zac's character's died. The game made a sound of, wirl… wirl…wirl…woo, and lights flashed off and on. The screen faded to black.

Zac pounded on the video game as young men do. "That's not fair, we were getting reading to level up."

"Zac take it easy." Mom prompted.

"Yeah Zac don't break the machine." Zoe smiled knowing she could get away with the comment with Mom at her side.

Zac still threw her a dirty look.

"Hi everybody." Said Steven with Scott at his side. "Let's go have a basketball contest. That way we can all take turns."

They all knew that Dad was the king of playing *HORSE*. But what the heck, all Dad's needs to win once in a while. The family went over to a bank of basketball Arcade games, called *Pop-A—Shot*. A furious fifteen minutes went by and sure enough, Steven won, but only by a narrow margin. Zac only lost by three points the young lad had been greatly improving on his game.

In a mom voice, "The time now is getting late, it's about nine o'clock.

"Time to head out." Dad agreed trying to round everybody up.

On the way out of the Arcade the youths spied Ultimate Mortal Kombat 5 and argued their way into playing a few games. Patiently the adults stood around, talking and let them play.

Just as Zoe and Zac wanted to start another game, Mom stepped in.

She announced, "It's getting late, and you guys have had plenty."

"But Mom, Zac started to plead. "Just one more game?"

"Yea Mom, one more game---please." Zoe added.

Mom put her foot down. "Enough is enough, beside we need to get back to the room, we have two dogs to walk before bedtime."

"That's final. Time to get to our room kids."

Agreeing Scott, "Let's round it up. Time to say goodnight,"

The youths shut up, because they could not argue about two dogs, especially since one is a puppy. Back to their rooms the Lund's went. Scott to his room, which was just down the hall from Zoe and Zac's room with their parents.

Later that night before bedtime, the Lund youths were walking down a path between two rolls of Palm trees , Stopping, Zoe stood patiently holding a poop bag as Thunder did his business. Zac slowed down and made a loop with Rosie back to Zoe. Rosie sat on point.

"What are you and Mom planning to do with Thunder?" Zac asked.

Zoe replied, "I'm not sure but when we get to the room we can ask Mom."

Scratched his chin thinking, "Somebody must be his owner. He looks like a purebred Golden Retriever. That means he must of cost money to someone.

Finishing up Thunder went over to sit down by Rosie.

"What if he just got lost in the storm and has no owners?" Zoe stated already knowing the answer.

"The owners will eventually turn up and claim him Zoe."

"I know bro, but I might want to keep pretending a bit longer and keep having fun with him."

They looked at Thunder sitting there his tail wagging, he sneezed and that made Rosie bark. Zoe and Zac both laughed.

A voice called out, again and again. A boy of maybe fifteen or sixteen walked by. "My dog is lost, have you seen any stray dogs around here?"

Zoe heart sank, but she gave an honest answer. "This puppy is a stray."

"Nice dog." The boy stopped and he petted Thunder's head. Who yipped.

Zoe felt so sad, no more puppy. Inside Zac worried about his sister. He put his hand on her shoulder.

"But this isn't my dog, my dog is a black Labrador. Have you seen him?"

"No! I have not." Zoe almost felt tears of joy.

"Okay let me know." The young man wandered off calling out the name, Sheena! Shenna! Come here Sheena." He figure disappeared down the path. His voice becoming merely an echo.

Squatting down, Zoe petted Thunder. "That's a close call Zac."

"I know sis, maybe it's wake up call to prepare you."

Frowned and in a snotty voice Zoe, "Maybe I don't want a wakeup call. Just leave me and Thunder alone. "Let's get back to our room. "I'm sure Dad will have popcorn ready.

"Popcorn, now were talking."

"Come then Zac lets go." Said Zoe wanting to leave before someone else would see Thunder.

Back to the room they went, where Zoe could at least have nice dreams. Zac paused in the lobby with Rosie looking at the signs on the whiteboard. He squinted his eyes on a particular message.

It said.

Wanted: Missing Golden Retriever puppy

Looking at the sign made Zoe's heart pang.

Zac stared at his sister. For a young man he withheld his tongue and kept his mouth shut. He could give his sister Zoe one more night of happiness.

CHAPTER 14

DAY 5

"You need to leave this soon Dad? But you just got here. Can't you stay one more day—please." The look on Zoe's eyes could melt an ice cube.

"Sorry honey, remember we missed a day due to the airplanes mechanical problems." Dad leaned downward to give her a hug.

"I know, but can't you just reschedule your flight back. I will even tolerate Zac another day or two if you stay." Zoe hugged her Dad.

Dad resisted laughing at that comment.

Mom joined in on, *pick on Dad*. She grabbed his other arm and squeezed it. "Can't you stay? Just one more day?"

Zoe and Lori both said, "Pleeeease!" Then Mom and Zoe kissed Dad on the cheeks.

Steven pushed away the women half-heartedly. "Hey that's not fair, the two of you teaming up on me. I would if I could, but I have a meeting Monday morning and so does Scott."

"Did I hear my name?" Asked Scott sitting in a chair playing Fortnite with Zac sitting in the next chair.

"They are giving me a rough time about going back to the States." Steven stated, "We both have meetings that are scheduled."

Shaking his head, Scott admitted, "Sadly that's true, or I would stay here for a month. But as they say, duty calls."

Steven had to agreed. "That's true, a park ranger and a border agent have many duties and responsibilities.

Looking at Scott in surprise, Zac paused the game. "You're going? Somehow I thought you would find a way to say an extra day or two."

"I wish I could nephew. You can stay here, and fly back with your mother, but that's not what your Dad and myself can do. We have both responsibilities." Scott felt sad about leaving his nephew and niece so soon.

It's amazing how dogs sense things, Rosie went over to Scott and nuzzled her snout on Scott's massive thigh. Her big brown eyes looked at Scott and she wagged her tail. Scott rubbed her nose and scratched Rosie's ears. She whimpered softly. Which got Thunder going, making a little growl in his small throat, he jumped up and ran around the motel room in circles.

"Thunder calm down—now!" Zoe bent over to catch him.

Thunder knocked over a garbage can, popcorn kernels spilled out from the opened popcorn bags. The puppy then jumped on the bed, grabbed a pillow with his razor sharp puppy teeth and whipped it around as he growled. Life is a game to puppy's, and all the world is their playground. Zoe dived at Thunder, he leaped to the floor and scurried under another bed. Zoe got up laughing.

"Zac." Zoe pointed to the other side of the bed.

Zac went over and leaned over the bed.

Zoe yelled, Boo!"

She grabbed at Thunder. He raced to the other side of the bed, smack right into Zac's hands.

"Gotcha." Zac scooped up a mass of cute squirming fur.

Looking at her two children, Lori said. "While you're at it, you two can take the dogs for a walk before we go the airport.

"Mom, we already walked them once this morning." Zac complained which Zoe agreed with.

Mom insisted, waving her finger. "You know how small a puppy's bladder is. Walk—Dogs--Now."

"Okay—Mom." Zac grumbled.

Getting up and in her high voice, Zoe called out to the dogs. "Want to go for a walk?"

Rosie leaped up to her feet and shook herself. She grabbed the leash off the table and put it in her mouth. Then Rosie carried the leash over and stood by the door. Zac carried Thunder over to the door, set him down and put a leash on him.

Steven added, "You two be back in half an hour, we don't want to be late for the airport. Remember we have to clear Customs flying back to the U.S."

"Don't worry about us Dad." Zac said heading to the door.

"We will be right back." Zoe reassured them.

"Okay take care and be right back." Mom called out with a smile.

The two youths went down the hallway and exited the Hotel Capybara to the parking lot. The tropical sun greet them brightly with beams of sunshine and waves of heat. They crossed a pavement so hot it would have burnt their feet, if they had no shoes on. The dogs moved briskly to get to the grass field on the far side of the lot. They slowed down and did their business, watering the trees so to speak. The youths walked the dogs around for a while and stopped to let the dogs sniff around frequently.

In the back of Zac's mind, he remembered seeing the missing dog poster from last night. *Where had he seen it?*

Zoe tugged on Thunder's leash. "C'mon boy, we don't have all day. Let's go."

A puppy like Thunder had other ideas. A small iguana, about half a meter long scurried by Thunder who yipped and barked. Surprisingly the puppy yanked so hard that Zoe dropped the leash and off went the puppy.

"Oh no!" cried out Zoe as she grabbed for the leash being dragged across the field.

Barking and straining on her leash, Rosie wanted to play chase. Zac's knuckles became white from trying to hold onto the leash of the large powerful collie. Zoe chased after the troublesome puppy. Taking off in pursuit, Zac and Rosie went after them. Thunder ran like lightning, out distancing Zoe through the field, nipping at the iguana's tail as it slithered under a rock. The dog pawed at an opening under the large rock. Thunder got smart and ran to the other side.

The iguana's head popped out from under the other side of the boulder. If an iguana could show surprise this one did, it's eyes grew larger, it's tongue flicked out. It couldn't squeeze backward, so it dashed forward. Thunder barked and bit it's tale. The iguana made a noise similar to a sneeze. It tried to shake its tail, but the puppy's jaws were strong and stubborn. Thrashing about in the weeds and grass, it became a battle of fur and scales. The iguana bit at

Thunder and missed--twice. Growling up a storm Thunder keep its grip with sharp baby primary teeth.

By now Zoe had caught up with the two combatants. They were now rolling about in the weeds, Zoe stood there unsure what to do. The lizard finally nipped Thunder with its sharp teeth designed to tear apart plants. Thunder whimpered in pain, but he stubbornly won't let go of the reptile's tail.

"Stop! Quit biting—now!" Zoe cried out like the iguana could understand English. "Don't bite my dog."

The two tussled and rolled around, kicking up dirt and sand. Zoe frowned, worried the iguana would injure the puppy. Zac and Rosie had arrived. Zac wasn't sure what to do either. Standing there, he scratched his head. Tugging and straining at her leash, Rosie attempted to get at the lizard. Zac didn't know if Rosie would make things better or worse.

"What do I do Zac?"

"I don't know. I wish Mom was here. Being a veterinarian, she would know what to do."

"Well Mom's not here, we are." Zoe looked down at the leash attached to Thunder.

"Zac give me your leash and hold Rosie by the collar."

Instantly Zac knew what Zoe would going to do. Siblings can think alike at times. Unhooking the leash, he grabbed the dog's collar and tossed the leash to Zoe. "Stay Rosie--stay."

The lizard snapped it's teeth at Thunder as he whipped the reptiles tail back and forth with his small, but powerful jaws. Zoe whipped the leash, and the hook hit the iguana on the head with a *thunk*. Zoe grabbed Thunder's leash and tugged it as hard as she could. The two animals separated, the lizard hissed and bolted into a tall patch of weeds.

Dropping the leash, Zoe wrapped her arms around Thunder. "Are you okay you brave silly dog?"

Zac came over and leashed up Rosie. Rosie whimpered and put her snout on Thunder's back. Thunder yipped and made a soft bark.

"Zoe look! Zac pointed to Thunder's left flank.

Noticing the bite, Zac touched a small amount of red staining the puppy's fur. He wiped his finger in the grass.

"Oh no, my poor puppy." Zoe exclaimed. She stood up, her fists clenched. "Where is that lizard? I am going to get him for hurting my dog. It will never bite another dog when I get through with him."

"Wait till Mom hears about this. It's your fault the dog got loose and got hurt."

"Zac, don't you dare tell Mom. It was an accident, that's all." Zoe face whitened.

"Okay sis, we figure something else out. But the look on your face was great."

Snarling, Zoe mumbled some choice words about brothers.

Zac ignored her, which prevented sibling fighting and bent over to examine the wounded puppy. "It's mostly a few scratch's Zoe. We can clean him up and hope nobody will know the difference."

Relieved Zoe said, "That would be great Zac…thanks."

"Let's go find some towels and water and see what we can do."

"What can you two do?"

Zoe and Zac spun at the sound of a familiar voice.

"Oh no, It's Mom." Zoe said in a whisper that could hardly be heard.

"A… nothing Mom. Zac answered.

"Nothing what?" Asked Dad.

"Well, it's just the Thunder got dirty and hurt trying to crawl under a rock." Zac responded.

"Let me see the dog." Mom leaned over the puppy to examine it. "Hmmmm."

"What is it Lori, is Thunder okay." Scott voice boomed.

Oh, no the whole family is here. We are in so much trouble. Zoe fidgeted about while Mom checked out the dog.

"These are bite marks, not scrapes from a rock or a stone. What is going on here?" Mom's tone rose as she talked. "Did Thunder get in a fight?!?"

"Not exactly, he chased an iguana." Zac tried to explain. "He kinda caught it."

Dad repeated, "He chased an iguana and kinda caught it?"

"Yeah that's it." Zac said.

"And the rest of the story young man?" Mom said, like she was asking if Zac had swiped some cookies or candy."

Zoe stepped in defending her brother. "It's my fault Mom, I was walking the puppy, he saw a lizard and bolted for it. Thunder is surprisingly strong for a puppy and yanked the leash out of my hand. He took off and chased the iguana under a rock and bit the tail. That mean old lizard bit Thunder back."

Zac butted in, "The dog did get loose, Zoe hit it reptile with the leash and got Thunder free. She sort of saved the puppy. It's like she's a hero."

Uncharacteristically, Zac held Zoe's hand. Zoe looked at her brother in shock, awe, and surprise.

"We were just checking him out and everybody should up. I think there are only a few scratches." Zac added.

Zoe agreed, "That's right, but I'm not a hero like Uncle Scott. I'm just protecting my pets from harm, just like you taught us Mom."

Running her fingers through the fur and over the dog's skin. "It does look superficial, nothing serious. Iguanas do have sharp teeth. We should be able to get him cleaned up and he will be fine."

Steven said, "We came to check on you guys since it's been over a half an hour. Some of us do have a plane to catch."

"In this world we wanted to make sure that everybody is safe." Scott added, always on the lookout for trouble.

"We will get Thunder back to the room and get him clean and patched up." Said Lori, the doctor.

"Thank God Mom, we were worried for a moment." Said a relived Zoe.

Sighing, Zac let out a breath he did not know he was holding in. "That's great news. No harm, no problem."

Dad voiced his opinion. "It seems like we need to practice our training and walking the dog exercises."

"Okay." Zoe and Zac said at the same time.

A voice call out, "Hey, nobody move."

The Lund's turned and looked and saw a family of three. A man, woman and a young girl approached them. The girl gasped and rushed over to Thunder. Zac and Zoe blocked her off.

"That's my dog! Let me at him." The young girl of eight or nine cried out.

Zoe disagreed, "No he's my dog, I found him. He got lost in a storm."

"My sister Zoe did find him after a storm."

The girl argued, "He is my dog, and he did get lost in the storm." She had a tear in the corner of her eye.

"We have had 'lost dog' posters up everywhere." Said the father.

"Our daughter has been a wreck missing her dog." The mother sated.

Wincing, Zac remembered seeing them.

"I'm sorry about Thunder, Zoe."

Zoe grabbed her brothers arm not knowing what to do. This time Zac did not pull away from his sister.

The girl broke out crying as she pointed at the puppy's wounds. "Look he's hurt! You hurt my dog. You are BAD people!"

The father shook his head and pulled out his cellphone. His voice became loud and furious. "I'm going call the Policia and report that you stole our dog and injured him. You will all be arrested when I am through!"

Stay turn for the exciting conclusion and prepare to bail out the Lund family from jail!

CHAPTER 15

The Lund's were stunned to say the least by the father's words.

Speaking first, Zoe raised her voice, "I did not steal your dog, and I would never steal anybody's dog. I love dogs and we gave Thunder a home and took good care of him."

"He's hurt and wounded." The mother pointing at the puppy said. "That's not taking care of a dog. Shame on you!"

Momma Lund reacted. "My children are good children, they wouldn't harm a dog or any animal for that matter. Don't you say shame on them. We found the dog, rescued him and gave him shelter till we could find the owners. The dog was injured by accident on this morning's walk. I will check him out and have him fixed up in no time at all."

It became a battle of the parents.

The girl's mother snapped back. "Like I buy that pack of lies. We had signs everywhere you must have seen at least one of them. You say you can fix him up? What are you a veterinarian?

In a professional tone. "As a matter of fact, I am an exotic animal Doctor and veterinarian.

The mother frowned so hard her eyebrows became one. "That's a hard one to swallow, that you're a vet. There is money to be made on dognapping."

Stomping her right foot, Lori barked back, "Are you calling me a liar."

"It seems that way." The mother took a step forward.

Lori actually clenched her fists, so did the mother.

Trying to avoid more trouble, Steven stepped between the two women. "It's true, my wife is a known around the world as a veterinarian. You can google her, Dr. Lorelei Lund. My name by the way is Steven, and this is Zac and Zoe."

Steven might as well have been talking to a wall. The mother ignored Steven.

The little girl tried to hold back tears. "He's my dog and his name is Cookie, because he is the color of cookie dough. "Here Cookie, come here."

Responding to the girl's voice, the puppy yipped, barked and pulled at his leash trying to get to the girl. Firmly Lori held the leash. The girl ran toward the puppy, but Zoe intercepted her. The girl pressed forward. Zoe stood in her way. Zac resisted smiling, for he knew his sister could take her out in a heartbeat, with her martial arts training.

Standing there feeling helpless and quite guilty, He could kick himself for not mentioning the sign he saw last night.

Zoe crossed her arms. The girl tried to push past Zoe, you may as well of told a mountain to move. The girl pouted and bit her lower lip. Zoe glanced at the girl to the puppy then back at the girl. Shaking her head slowly Zoe gently moved backward toward the puppy, her eyes moist, her lips drawn together tightly. Zoe let the girl push past her and girl fell to her knees hugging the small dog so tightly he yipped. With her eyes overflowing with tears, Zoe turned around and placed her hand on the girl's shoulder and then kneeled beside her, both girls burst out in waves of tears. They hugged each other with the puppy trapped between them.

As she released the leash, Lori not to cry herself as she backed away.

The adults stood in silence at this tender moment of the two girls and the dog. Moving over by her husband, Lori took Steven's hand. Uncle Scott placed his hand on Zoe's shoulder.

Between tears and crying Zoe, said, "I sorry that I tried to stop you. It's so easy to love the dog, I…"

Rosie barked and broke the silence.

The father spoke up showing his phone a picture to his wife. "It's true Dr Lund is on Google. They are legit." He cleared his throat, "Can we all start over. I am John Bloom, this is my wife Connie…and this girl is my daughter Elizabeth. We call her Beth for short.

The girls were still hugging each other, their drops of tears staining the ground. Rosie closed in whining and stuck her long snoot in between the girls. Zoe straightened up and petted Rosie. Beth kept hugging Cookie. Her tears started to slowed down, and her hand rubbed her nose.

"I should say thank you for finding…" Beth sniffled, "Cookie and for keeping him safe."

"Not a problem." Zoe replied trying not to cry anymore.

It look like the crisis has passed.

Zoe went over and stood by Mom and Dad, Mom handed her a tissue. The Bloom's went over and placed their hands on Beth. Then John left the group and talked to the Lund's.

"I want to thank you and apologize for doubting, it's a harsh world and you never know nowadays what to expect." He pulled out his wallet, "I would like to offer a reward for finding Cookie. Here Zoe." He had a fistful of peso's."

Solemnly, Zoe said, "No thank you sir."

"No? You don't' want a reward?" John asked puzzled.

"No, it's because Thunder…er I mean Cookie found us. He somehow got into our room to escape the storm. He hid under the bed till we returned to our room that was demolished. All we had to do was take care of him."

Zoe didn't mention buying all the stuff for the puppy. "Is that okay Mom, no reward."

Mom promptly agreed. "That's right, we can't take money. In fact, Mister Bloom, we have some extra food, and you can keep the leash and collar."

"That's kind and generous of you. You deserve your five star Google rating Dr. Lund. But I would like to reward you in some way, perhaps if not money perhaps a gift to your wonderful daughter...Zoe. Correct?"

"I'm okay, just take good care of the puppy." Zoe said, her eyes were still moist."

Beth came over with Cookie on the leash. "Thank you, thank you." She gave Zoe a half hug. She whispered into Zoe's ear. "My Dad has lots of money and is a toy designer. Take him up on his offer."

Zoe shrugged her shoulders, why not? "Maybe I could take a small gift."

John smiled broadly, "I am a doll designer and work for a large company that manufactures L.O.L. dolls. How about I design a Zoe L.O.L. doll with your parents' permission."

All that Zoe could manage to say, "Wow!"

"We might say…yes," Said Steven. Let's trade info and emails. Then talk about it, okay?"

"With pleasure and we would have to talk a few legal details."

"Of course we would." Said Dad wanting to be protective.

"That would be awesome Zoe, you very own L.O.L. doll." Said Beth. "Hey Dad?"

"Yes, what dear?"

I might need my own L.O.L. also."

"If we have two dolls can they have pet capybara's also?" Zoe asked.

Clapping her hands together in glee, Beth stated, "Great then we can have twin L.O.L. pets."

Everybody laughed and chuckled except for John, he had opened his big mouth and had to deal with it. Emails and phone numbers were traded, and the Lund's had to leave. They had a plane to catch.

"Goodbye Beth, take care of Cookie."

"Goodbye to you Zoe. Thanks' and you take good care of your dog, Rosie."

As if on cue, Rosie went over and nuzzled with Cookie, the two had become friends.

Maybe a dog's best friend is another dog?

There is fog and there is fog. A heavy fog had rolled into the Airport, engulfing the sun and daylight. The thick mist swirling and moving around, in some ways the world seemed covered in a mist that was pure magic. The murky clouds touched the ground.

Observing the inclement weather, Uncle Scott said, "I think I remember a joke. What do you call a fog over Italy?"

No one answered, even though Steven knew the family joke.

Smirking and in an Italian accent Scott said. "It's a big-a-mist."

Steven and Lori laughed, Zoe and Zac sort of laughed as if they understood it.

A loudspeaker blared, "All departures will be delayed for two hours."

"That's a relief." Steven said half-jokingly. "Nothing like hurrying up then having to wait.

Lori grinned. "Okay, but I didn't want to wait here all day." She said in a teasing way. "… or get stuck with you two men."

Steven pretended to object. "Hey! There are worse people to get stuck with."

Waiving her hands in the air, Mom gave in. "Oh I suppose so…but we have to prepare for our own return flight. And as all good pilots do I need to run a complete instrument check today on our jet plane."

Zac questioned, "I fly back with you and Zoe correct?"

Making a face, "Mom, do we have to take Zac with us?"

"Yes dear you flew with me down here. Zac has the right to fly back with us."

"That's right sis, unless you want to fly back with Dad? Then I can fly back with just Mom and Rosie."

Zoe put her hands on her hips. "No way! Rosie is my dog, and I will be the one to fly back with him. Not you!"

Her brother grimaced, "But Mom, I want to fly…"

Breaking up the almost sibling fight, Scott slapped his bronzed hands together, like he swatted a mosquito.

WHACK!

"Listen up you two." You both go back with Mom, and I get to fly back with your father. Right!?!"

For once Zac and Zoe stood silent. Mom and Dad exchanged looks, Dad gave Mom the thumbs up. Casually Scott looked at his weather app on his phone. "The weather front is passing by followed by what looks like a light rain. We should than be good to go."

292

"Nothing like tropical delays to keep you off schedule." Steven added shaking his head at the weather and his two children. "I should still be able to keep meeting tomorrow morning. I'll just be minus two hours of sleep."

"Soothingly, Lori consoled her husband, "You will be okay Steven, just have an extra cup of coffee in the morning and you will be good to go."

Lori touched Uncle Scott's shoulder. "Thanks for coming here to be with us. I know you keep such a busy schedule."

"Not a problem Lori, you have to balance work and family, that's what our dad always said. I needed a break from the U.S. Border Patrol anyway. It was great to here and see you guys, tomorrow is back to work."

Abruptly Scott's phone rang. It sounded like the 1960's Batman ringtone. He took out his phone and scanned the screen. His amber colored eyes narrowed, his lips tightened. "Excuse me everybody I need to take this." Scott walked off a few meters speaking in hushed undertones.

Moving over, Zoe hugged Dad. "Thanks for coming I'm starting to miss you already."

"Thanks pumpkin, sometimes you say the sweetest things. Then other times…"

"Oh Dad." Zoe pulled away playfully.

293

"Have a good and safe flight Dad."

"I will son." The two Lund men fist bumped. Steven looked at the time on his smartphone. "Great, now I get the pleasure of going through security and clearing customs." Steven looked at his family. "Time for a Lund huddle."

The four Lund's gathered up in a semi-circle.

"Listen up," Said Steven, his eyes focused on his children. "God bless and protect our family! Mexico is a dangerous place. Be on your guard and pay attention to everything and everyone around you. Be cautious and watchful, without showing fear or anxiety. Never accept any candy or gifts from strangers. You know the safety drill, yell, kick, scratch or bite. You have Martial art training also. But don't fight unless it's the last resort."

Both children said, "Yes Dad."

Steven said, "And…"

Smiling, Zoe loudly added, "And listen and obey Mom."

"That's right, always obey your parents and beware of strangers." Zac added.

Lori asked, "Anything else?"

Zoe thought for a moment. "Yes, when we ask to do something." Zac added "We wait and get permission first before we do it."

Steven nodded, "Sounds like we have some decent kids Lori."

"I guess we'll keep them." Lori tried not to smile.

Scott walked up, "Keep who?"

No one said a word.

"I might have some news, maybe not so good."

Everyone looked at Scott.'

"I can't fly back with Dad, I got called out on assignment. There is an emergency at the Texas border involving a vicious drug Cartel. Zac you get to take my plane ticket, its' too late to refund or cancel it."

Zac groaned out loud and Zoe smiled thinking, *I get to fly home with Mom alone.*

All stories must have a beginning and an end. This is the end of the line for you the reader.

Wait for the further adventures of the Lund Family Mysteries.

THE END

Meet **Dr. Richard A. Olson**, a doctor now turned writer.

A man of two worlds, Richard learns from the past and writes about the future. Dr. Olson grew up training as an athlete, martial artist, and bodybuilder. He loves music and was a professional rock drummer. Richard is an avid reader of Batman comics, books, and Pulp magazines. He is passionate about film de noir black and white movies from the 1930's and 1940's, and vintage TV shows.

The kids call him **Dr. Batman!** A Batcave in his basement supports his nickname. Richard has been a lifelong Batman fan since he was seven years old. Batman is almost believable, he has no superpowers and has to rely on his brain and skills. Also being a Billionaire does not hurt. Batman is the world's greatest detective.

Richard has a diverse passion for the future and where it leads. To stay green and fresh, he watches movies about Sci-Fi, superheros, and modern action heroes. Richard listens to and enjoys Audible books of all types.

Another facet for Richard is being outside. He enjoys bicycling, bonfires, golf, hiking, and most of all swimming or anything in, under, or by the water. Everywhere Richard has lived is by the water. He lived on an island in the Mississippi River, on an Illinois River beach, by three different lakes, and near a pond that had frogs the size of ducks. No, he didn't croak.

Currently Dr. Olson is a Chiropractic Physician and Acupuncturist. The author, his wife Angela, their two children and a giant white dog live by twin lakes outside of Peoria, Illinois. Richard was raised in Church and loves God. He also knows that God has a sense of humor, Richard looked into a mirror and they both laughed.

Series: Nick Stihl, Private Investigator

Scott Lund, the Border Agent

Lund Family Mysteries YA

www.ingramcontent.com/pod-product-compliance
Lightning Source LLC
Chambersburg PA
CBHW070558260626
47161CB00002B/645